The Am

Also by Christopher Bowden

The Amber Maze

Christopher Bowden

LANGTON & WOOD

Copyright © Christopher Bowden 2018
First published in 2018 by Langton & Wood
73 Alexandra Drive, London SE19 1AN
http://www.christopherbowden.com

Distributed by Gardners Books, 1 Whittle Drive, Eastbourne,
East Sussex, BN23 6QH
Tel: +44(0)1323 521555 | Fax: +44(0)1323 521666

The right of Christopher Bowden to be identified as the author of
the work has been asserted herein in accordance with the Copyright,
Designs and Patents Act 1988.

All the characters in this book are fictitious and any resemblance to
actual people, living or dead, is purely imaginary.

British Library Cataloguing in Publication Data
A catalogue record for this book is available from the British Library.

ISBN 978-0-9555067-5-8

Typeset by Amolibros, Milverton, Somerset
www.amolibros.co.uk
This book production has been managed by Amolibros
Printed and bound by T J International Ltd, Padstow, Cornwall, UK

One

Hugh Mullion sank to the bench at the back of the cottage and looked across the fields to the hills beyond. They were bathed in the warm golden light of early evening. The bench itself was in shade but the still-warm air and the buzzing of bees about the lavender made him feel sleepy. Or perhaps it was the pint of Curate's Winkle he had downed for old times' sake at the Talbot Arms in the village. Either way, it was a while before he hauled himself up, went inside the cottage and found what was there.

Hugh had been in Dorset a couple of days and was due to be joined in a couple more by his wife, Kate. A week together at Lenten Cottage, a single-storey building of brick and flint with a broad tiled roof starred with lichen. It lurked in the landscaped grounds of a larger house, known as The Hall, but was well out of sight of it. This guaranteed privacy and seclusion for tenants of the cottage while ensuring that the owner, Mrs Butterfield, was on hand if circumstances required.

Even Kate, not one for sentiment, had said the place looked charming as she looked over his shoulder while he worked his way through potential candidates. Lenten Cottage, they read on the website, was named for the hellebores that put on a spectacular show in the late winter and early spring. If proof were needed, photographs showed a fuzz of flower beneath a leafless hazel tree: plum and dusky pink, slate and butter-yellow, cream and brilliant white, some plain, others speckled or freckled. But now, in high summer, there was little to see but a mass of leathery leaves interspersed with ferns in the shady area bordering the path that led up to The Hall.

Kate did not fail to spot that the village of Newton Manville in which the cottage lay was only two miles from the town of Okeminster and just a little further from Newton FitzPosset, the village she had come to know too late.

"Dorothy country," she said quietly. "A long time ago now."

"It's over ten years since she died," he said. "And five since George joined her. I thought we might have a look when we're down there."

When Hugh returned from the Talbot Arms, he went directly to the rear of the cottage, taking the path down the side, without having to pass through the interior and open the French windows. He therefore went back the way he had come before unlocking the front door and pushing into the open-plan sitting-cum-dining room. And then he saw the thing. He could scarcely avoid it. To the right of the fireplace, a large winged armchair that had not been there this morning. It looked wholly out of place, a cuckoo in the nest. The careful arrangement of the existing furniture had been disrupted to accommodate it, rucking the colourful kilims that covered the flagstone floor.

His first instinct was to march up to the main house and ask Mrs Butterfield to have the chair removed. But he was having a rest from the dynamic and confrontation wasn't really his style. Better to keep on the right side of Mrs B. There was probably a simple explanation. He looked round for a note but found nothing. Perhaps a casual word after breakfast if their paths happen to cross.

He went over to the CD player and pressed 'Play'. Miles Davis again. He wandered into the kitchen to the strains of 'Summertime' and returned with a glass of rosé. He glanced at the chair. Surreptitiously, almost as if he did not want the chair to know he was looking. It had a certain elegance and style, he conceded, and was clearly a quality piece, even if the upholstery was faded and frayed in places. He contemplated the fabric. Sea-green, was it? Aquamarine? Teal? It was hard to say. Easy on the eye, though. Rather restful.

He sat in the chair and settled himself. It was comfortable, very comfortable, and the cushion pleasingly padded. He imagined sitting beside a blazing fire on a winter's evening, the wings trapping the heat and protecting from draughts. But why was there only one chair? Didn't these things come in pairs, one for each side of the fireplace?

The sudden chirrup of a mobile phone interrupted his thoughts. It was his phone but where it was he could not be sure. As he leapt up, coins slipped from his pocket and down the side of the chair. He ran to the kitchen and then to the bedroom, where he pounced on the instrument lying on the bed. Hugh was not at ease with mobile phones and only had one because Kate insisted. He didn't share her view of the merits of being reachable at any time of day and night and felt that getting away should mean just that. The length of the conversation with Kate rather reinforced his view, much as he was looking forward to seeing her the day after tomorrow. And the twins? He missed Eleanor and Rosie, of course; rather more than he let on but Kate assured him they were having a whale of a time at the camp in Norfolk. It was the first occasion in their nine years they had been away from home for more than a night.

The account of his day he gave to Kate did not include the sudden appearance of the chair to which he now returned to retrieve a pocketful of change. A few coins were caught between the cushion and the arm and these he lifted deftly one by one before removing the cushion itself. Others nestled in the narrow crack along the side of the seat. He picked out several more but inserting his fingers into the crack to recover the rest simply widened it, enabling a fifty-pence piece and three one-pound coins to slide from view.

He cursed and wished he had thought earlier of fetching the tongs from the kitchen drawer. He tried to push his hand in further but the gap was too tight and he could barely move his fingers. He drew his hand out and wondered whether he should approach the problem from a different direction by taking a knife to the bottom of the chair. But he could hardly start damaging Mrs Butterfield's property for the sake of a few coins and what if she found out?

'Summertime' had long finished but other tracks from *Porgy and Bess* formed a melodious backdrop to his conversation with Kate and his attempts to retrieve the money, finally mocking him for the loss of the coins with a reprise of 'Gone'. He decided to try again, without musical accompaniment, by straddling the arm of the chair and placing one knee close to the edge of the seat so that his weight would make the gap at the side open wider. The plan was partly successful in that he could now slip his hand in deeper and feel around. The coins remained out of reach but his fingertips touched something else. He managed to grip it between two fingers. At first it resisted his attempts to lift it out, as if held or caught in the clutch of another hand. And then suddenly it came with a jerk: the remnants of a luggage label, a small key dangling from it provocatively.

He put the cushion back on the chair and sat down, turning the key over and over and wondering what it was for. Slim, a couple of inches long, if that, dull but not rusty and with an oval eye at one end through which the string of the label was threaded. A small cupboard or cabinet? The case of a grandfather clock? A box of some sort? He looked round the room for ideas, not that there was any reason to suppose a connection with the cottage since the key must have slipped down the side long before the chair was dumped here.

He leaned over to switch on the standard lamp and examined the label, or what remained of it, in the crisp white light. The label was grubby, battered and torn but he could make out some letters in faded violet ink:

LION
HIS
THE G

Whatever else the label may have said had been lost when it was ripped. It offered no clue to the function of the key or where it had come from. Intriguing, though. Perhaps Mrs Butterfield knew something about it. She may even have lost the key herself. And it was a good way of raising the sudden appearance of the chair. He would have a word with her in the morning.

Two

*H*e huffed his way up to The Hall, a large house of gold-grey stone set well back from the road that led to the centre of the village. Vanessa Butterfield was in the garden. A stocky red-faced woman with straw-coloured hair, she was bending over the rose border with secateurs and a trug.

"I'm dead-heading my Sexy Rexy," she said, "and cutting a few for the house. Wonderful fragrance." She thrust one of the soft pink rosettes at Hugh and invited him to smell it. Before he could reply, she said, "I like to mix them with Darcey Bussell." She nodded at the deep crimson roses in full flower nearby. "Is all well at the cottage?"

They adjourned to the kitchen, where he produced the key and explained how he had found it.

"Good heavens. I'd forgotten the chair. It shouldn't be there at all. A thousand apologies. I was just seeing how it looked when I was called away. Barry must have locked up after me. I'll get him to remove it at once."

'Barry' was Mr Butterfield. Hugh was suspicious of

men called Barry, especially when the name was used alliteratively, and wondered at Vanessa's choice of partner. He kept his thoughts to himself. Instead, he assured her that the chair was a welcome and comfortable addition to the cottage and tried to focus her on the key that was swinging gently from the shred of label in his hand.

"Can't help, I'm afraid. I've not had the chair long. That's why I was trying it out. It'll need re-upholstering, wherever it ends up." She poured the coffee and pushed a jug of milk towards him. "I bought it in the sale at Nigel Gosling's antiques shop in Okeminster. You could try him if you want to find out more. Obviously, he'd have had no idea the key was there when he sold the chair to me but he should at least know where it came from."

Hugh parked his car in Market Square. The space was close to the remains of the market cross outside the Bear, the hotel where he stayed on his first visit to Okeminster all those years ago when he came to Dorset to see Dorothy Johnson in the neighbouring village of Newton FitzPosset. And on the opposite side of the square, the church of St John looming in the background, the corner where he had an unexpected sighting of her, chanting and waving a placard and ignoring the attempts of the police to move her on.

Nigel Gosling's shop was in Castle Street, a few minutes' walk away. It occupied gloomy double-fronted premises with that sense of stiffness and quiet formality characteristic of antiques shops of a certain sort found in country towns across the land. It was hardly welcoming but he had only come with a query, not to browse or buy. Perhaps Mrs Butterfield's name would do the trick.

The door juddered open. As he stepped on the mat inside, a piercing two-tone bell sounded from the back of the shop. A woman of indeterminate age and a girlish air appeared from behind a linen press. He could imagine her becoming skittish after a glass or two of Chardonnay at the Christmas party.

"Nigel's not here today," she said. "He's at a house sale in Shelborne Magna. So, it's just little me. All on my ownsome. I'm Sandra, by the way. Sandra Bodkin. Sharp by name but… not by nature."

He introduced himself and put the question.

"Let me have a look at my ledger." She opened a desk drawer, pulled out a hard-covered exercise book and flipped the pages. "Here we are. Mrs Vanessa Butterfield, The Hall, Newton Manville. A painting and two wing chairs. She had them delivered."

Two wing chairs? Where was the other one?

"Do you know where they came from, the chairs? We found a key down the side of one of them." He pulled the key from his pocket and showed it to her. "Someone may be wondering where it is. Unless you have anything from the same source it might open."

"I'm not sure where Nigel picked them up. Maybe a house clearance, maybe an auction. But I do know he was pleased to shift the chairs because they looked rather odd together, not being a proper match, and took up a lot of room." She put out a hand for the key and turned it over in her palm a few times as if hoping for a sudden insight or flash of recall. None came. "I can't think of anything in the shop it would fit. Give me your number and I'll ask Nigel to get in touch."

Hugh put away the supplies he had bought, broadly in line with Kate's instructions, on his way back from Okeminster and wondered if Mrs Butterfield was about. She had clearly been to the cottage in his absence because a large jug of roses had appeared on the dining table, filling the room with fragrance.

There was no sign of her at The Hall. Downstairs windows were shut tight and knocking or ringing at doors produced no response. The elusive Barry was no more in evidence than on previous occasions. Hugh had never met him.

At the back of the house, he spotted the tight ball of fur that was Mimolette, the Butterfields' ginger cat. She was under a garden table, taking advantage of a patch of shade. As he bent to stroke her, she stretched and yawned and ambled towards the outbuildings on the other side of the courtyard. She slipped through a door that was discreetly ajar. He followed and found himself inside a building thick with sawdust and cobweb. It was part workshop and part dumping ground for furniture and assorted household items. Mimolette was looking at him from the seat of a chair, apparently unconcerned that her fur clashed horribly with the paisley fabric, mustard, magenta and lime, in which it was upholstered.

It was the other wing chair, unmistakably the missing

companion of the one in the cottage, despite the hideously mismatched upholstery. Why would anyone have done it? The thought of the two together made him feel queasy but his eye was caught by something else. It was leaning against the side of the chair. He bent down to have a better look and gave a start of surprise. He recognised the picture straightaway. It was one of Lucy Potter's series of Turkish watercolours. He had first seen it on the wall of her studio in Dogberry Road only two doors away from where he and Kate used to live. At her Christmas show that year he bought two other pictures instead: *A Street in Bodrum* and *Sunset over Zonguldak*. He lent them later for her retrospective at Bainbridge and Murray in Cork Street.

He turned the picture over. A small printed label gave the title, *Market in Trabzon*, and the price, a considerable bargain by current standards. But no reference to gallery or framer or any other indication of provenance. He turned the picture back and wondered how it came to be here. Unlike Mimolette, who had jumped from her spot and run from the building, he did not hear Vanessa Butterfield's Volvo on the gravel at the front or the slamming of the car door.

"I thought we had burglars."

He wheeled round in fright and saw Mrs Butterfield standing at the doorway, arms akimbo. He spluttered an apology, citing roses (the jug in the cottage) and the cat (followed into the building). It sounded feeble but she was unperturbed.

"I see you've found the other chair. Repulsive in its

present livery but the pair were a snip, even allowing for the cost of re-covering. That picture came with them; I must decide what to do with it. I had a call from Nigel Gosling, by the way, wanting to check your bona fides. He said he'd give you a ring."

There was no sign of Sandra Bodkin. It was a man with sandy hair and half-moon glasses who appeared when the mat bell sounded. He was holding a wad of cloth in one hand and a tin of French polish in the other. He put them down, confirmed that he was indeed Nigel Gosling and greeted Hugh like a long-lost friend.

"They came from a woman in Newton FitzPosset. I'd intended to have them re-upholstered, both the same, and put them on the website. But my usual man's been ill and the other chap is up to his eyes. So I thought it best to shift them as they were as soon as I could. The woman was engaged in some serious downsizing before she moved. I can't think how she crammed so much into a small cottage."

"You had some other things from her?"

"Let's think. A mahogany wardrobe, a tea table and a couple of chests of drawers come to mind. All gone now."

"Anything that this key might have fitted?"

Nigel Gosling took it from him and examined it in the light of a lamp with a parchment shade.

"Not that I recall. No doors or drawers were locked anyway. Keys frequently go missing, of course. This one could have been lost down the side before the previous owner even acquired the chairs so it may not relate to anything of hers at all. The chairs clearly hadn't been re-covered in a long while. The label's pretty tatty – and how long since anyone used violet ink?"

"Any idea what the key is for?"

"Hard to be sure. A small cabinet or cupboard, perhaps, or possibly a glazed bookcase. It's a bit large for a tea caddy or a tantalus."

"Mrs Butterfield bought a picture at the same time as the chairs. Did that come from the same place? I ask because I know the artist, Lucy Potter."

"It arrived in the van with the other stuff but, to be honest, I don't recollect seeing it at the cottage at all. I only remember buying the furniture."

"Am I allowed to ask the woman's name?"

"I probably shouldn't give it without her permission. Professional ethics and all that, not that she's there anymore. Let's just say that her address was not unadjacent to January Cottage. Off School Lane."

Three

The village of Newton FitzPosset was much as he remembered it, the only noticeable change being the reversion of the Startled Ox to its former name, the Bell. He drove down the main street, slowing as he passed St Mary's, the church where the funerals of Dorothy Johnson and her husband George had taken place some five years apart. Even in the bright light of a summer's day it looked dull and depressing, a grumpy toad of a building squatting among dark yews.

He came to the wooden bus shelter at the junction with School Lane and turned left, continuing until he found the track leading to January Cottage. There was little to see. The cottage was set back well and largely hidden from view by high hedges. Just a glimpse of pale pink walls and a forget-me-not blue front door. A board near the gate declared that the property had been SOLD but there was no sign of the new occupiers and he was not ready to find out if they were at home.

He left the car where it was and made his way back on foot, keeping to the shade as best he could. Past the pub and into Bell Lane until he came to Bell Cottage, the Johnsons' old house. It hadn't changed at all. He wondered if Dorothy and George had known whoever it was that used to live at January Cottage. Not unlikely in a small village. But he did not linger long, recalling that he had promised Kate a visit to Newton FitzPosset, and headed back to the main street and the general store.

The shop looked empty. There were no customers about and no one behind the till. He was about to call out when a sudden explosion of laughter drew him to a small room at the back. It was lined with shelves that were crammed with balls of wool, arranged in a rainbow sequence. A robust woman with a shopping basket of the sort seen in French markets was standing with two others, who looked as though they worked in the place. One of them held a piece of paper and all of them turned when Hugh materialised in the doorway.

"The brass-cleaning rota for St Mary's," said the woman with the paper, as if in explanation for the outburst of mirth. "Can we help you?"

"I was looking for January Cottage. I seem to have mislaid it."

"That's Mrs Badingham's place," said the third member of the trio, a freckled girl with copper hair. "'Least it was. She's moved now."

"If it's Hester Badingham you want, I'm afraid you're three weeks too late," said the robust woman. "She's left us after more than twenty years. A distinctive person. We were sorry to see her go."

"Do you know where she went?"

"There was talk of her moving in with her daughter's family in London. Between you and me, she wasn't keen and I'm not sure how it was resolved."

"Rachel was worried about Hester living on her own in Dorset after dear Archie died," put in the rota woman. "She wanted her mother to be near them. Hester soldiered on as she always did and held out for quite a while but I think she was getting a bit apprehensive herself about the prospect of spending her declining years down here."

"She looked as fit as a fiddle," said the robust woman. "She was quite a bit younger than Archie, of course."

"If the new man's there today," said the freckled girl, "you could ask him. He may have a forwarding address."

He left the store with directions and a punnet of strawberries. He put the punnet in the car in School Lane and made for January Cottage. Another car was now parked carelessly in front of it, all but blocking access to the gate.

At the third ring, the door was pulled open with some force. A middle-aged man glared, his face much the same colour as the brick-red trousers sagging below his waist.

"Yes?"

"I was looking for Mrs Badingham."

"She's left," said the man. "As in moved away."

"Do you have her new address?"

"I've not a clue where she went. There's a stack of mail for her. I'll have to chuck it at this rate. I tried the agents who sold the house but they simply referred me to her solicitors. I think that goes beyond the call of duty."

That evening, Hugh went into the bedroom at Lenten Cottage, opened the drawer at the base of the wardrobe and removed the laptop he had not touched since he arrived. He took it to the dining table and went to the website he had used to track down old school friends a month or two ago. He found Hester Badingham easily enough but the only address given was the one she had just left. Perhaps not surprising. He decided to approach the problem from another angle. He sent an email and went outside to sit with a glass of wine and watch the sun slip below the trees that lined the tops of the encircling hills.

Lucy Potter's reply was waiting when he came in. She had checked her records. The watercolour *Market in Trabzon* had been sent some time ago to a Mrs Hester Badingham at January Cottage in Newton FitzPosset, near Okeminster, Dorset. She hoped that would help.

He groaned and hit the table, making the roses tremble in their jug. But as he was on the way to the kitchen the ping of the laptop signalled another incoming message. It was Lucy again. She had a different invoice address for the picture. A woman in London, whom she remembered had bought it as a present for her mother and asked her to send it direct as she and her family were going away.

He recognised the name of the street. It was only a

few minutes' walk from their old house in Dogberry Road. And, according to the website he had consulted before, the woman still lived there. The occupiers were listed as Rachel and Guy Broadbent. Why would Mrs Badingham dispose of a painting that was a present from her daughter? Apart from anything else, they would surely be seeing more of each other and might even be living under the same roof. Wherever she went, selling the picture was hardly saving space. Unlike the chairs and the other furniture she let go. Whether she had what was opened by the key was something else again.

Four

---

*I*t was Kate who made progress. Of a sort. She spotted the key on the mantelpiece during her tour of inspection. She picked it up by the shred of label and dangled it in front of him.

"What's this?"

She listened to his explanation and said,

"I see. So, you've discovered the name of the person who previously owned the chair but don't know where she lives or whether the key was hers or, even if it was, whether she still has what it opened. Surely, if she'd lost the key she'd have looked down the side of the chair herself."

"It had slipped right inside," he said plaintively. "I had a job retrieving it once I'd caught hold of the label."

"Maybe that's when the label was torn. It may be old and tatty but the tear looks quite fresh."

"You mean the rest of it could still be there," he said, suddenly perking up.

Hugh lay on the floor and pushed up the base of the

chair from underneath while Kate eased her hand down the side. Her fingers were long and slender and penetrated further than his.

"One comb. A Fox's glacier mint. The rest of your change. And the other half of the label. Feels like it got caught on a tack. You must have torn it yourself when you pulled out the key."

They adjourned to the dining table. The roses in the jug at one end were beginning to drop but the fragrance was still intense. He put the two parts of the label together:

LIONEL PYBUS
HIS BOX
THE GROVE

"At least we know what it opens – or used to open," she said. "For what that's worth. As for The Grove and Mr Pybus. Didn't you say her name was Badingham?"

"Her married name, yes. I'll need to research her family history."

"Why? I mean, where is this going?" She put an arm around his shoulder and said more gently, "I agree it's intriguing but we don't want it to develop into a full-blown Dorothy obsession."

"That was over ten years ago, not that I would call it an obsession. I was only trying to track her down to return the book. And neither of us could have guessed how it would turn out. But you may be right. If there was anything of interest in the box when the key was lost it would have been forced open, either then or later."

On the other hand, he did have the daughter's address in London. Perhaps he had omitted to mention that to Kate. Now all he needed was an excuse to get in touch with Rachel Broadbent.

Five

Hugh was sitting at his desk in the study at number twelve Falstaff Road, a large Victorian semi-detached house in a close-packed street of similar properties. From the window, pricks of light through the intervening trees marked the backs of neighbouring houses. After a week in Dorset he was feeling relatively relaxed, despite the prospect of a return to work in the morning. Kate still had a few days off before the girls went back to school and she resumed at the Centre for Natural Medicine where she practised as a homeopath four days a week.

For Hugh, it was the Commission for Built Heritage and Historic Landscapes in England, generally known as the Heritage Commission, a body which, against the drift of public policy over the years, had retained its name, structure and functions and continued to occupy office space in the West End. He had been promoted to the post of Director of Conservation Policy in his early thirties. This was considered young at the time but, ten years on, he was still there; the career pyramid had narrowed sharply and opportunities for advancement were few and far between. In truth, he was becoming bored with the daily routine and the unexpected arrival of Lionel Pybus and his key provided a welcome diversion.

A picture was leaning against the bookcase. It was the watercolour *Market in Trabzon*. Vanessa Butterfield had given it to him when he and Kate had trekked to The Hall to say their goodbyes and would accept no money for it.

"You know the artist and have others by her. I think you'll give it a better home."

He wanted to keep it and could have left it at that. But this was an opportunity to make contact with Rachel Broadbent and, through her, with her mother, Hester Badingham. A long shot, perhaps, but the nagging feeling persisted that the key he had found was the key to more than a box.

He wasn't much of a Facebook fan but sometimes amused himself by looking at the pages of people he knew or half-knew – just to see. The amount of detail varied, some baring their souls to all and sundry, others keeping their cards close to their chests. Rachel Broadbent came somewhere in between, he discovered. Her profile picture, set against the incongruous backdrop of giant cacti in an arid landscape, showed a youngish woman with dark straight hair, an open expression and smiling eyes. Not a bad start. Other details were sparse. He knew she was married anyway but not that her interests included travel and reading. She was a regular customer of Toad Books, her entry revealed, as he had been for a dozen years or more himself. Another point of connection that could come in useful.

He was so absorbed in his research that he did not hear Kate come into the study.

"Why are you stalking Rachel Broadbent?" she asked, not unpleasantly.

He jumped but recovered quickly. "Lucy mentioned her; she originally bought the picture that came from Mrs Butterfield. I was just wondering who she was."

"Rachel used to be a patient of mine. So I know rather more about her than I can tell you. Interesting case. Her girls go to the same school as ours; I see her at the gate from time to time. That profile picture was taken a while ago."

"Do you think I should tell her about the painting? It's almost come full circle. Perhaps a bit tactless if her mother didn't want it."

"Her mother?"

"Turns out she's none other than Our Lady of the Chairs, Hester Badingham. Lucy said the painting was a Christmas present."

Kate left the room and reappeared five minutes later looking smug.

"I found Rachel's number and gave her a ring. We're all going there for supper on Tuesday. It'll be just her and the girls; Guy's in New York. Don't forget to take the picture."

★

The Old Rectory was in a wide road lined with plane trees. It was separated from St Matthew's Church by a modern hall that was being used for a slimming class when the Mullions drew up.

"Guy's a merchant banker," said Kate as Hugh stared at the gothic pile looming between horse chestnuts in the grounds. The stock bricks of which the house was built, and recently cleaned by the look of it, gleamed butter yellow in the early evening sun, making the place warm and welcoming, a little less intimidating than it had appeared at first sight. A five-bar gate gave on to a sweep of gravel and the garage block beyond. The Mullions entered by a smaller gate squeezed between stone pillars and took the path leading to a pitch-roofed porch and the wide front door.

The girls whooped upstairs with Willow and Matilda, the Broadbents' daughters, while Rachel steered Kate towards the sitting room. Hugh loitered in the hall, admiring the stained glass in the triple window high above, the geometric tiles of the floor below awash with colour.

"That's the one!" said Rachel, flushing as he drew the watercolour from the carrier bag he had been clutching. She took the picture and held it to the light. "My mother was really upset when she realised it was missing; the cottage was in chaos, she said, while she sorted out what to keep and what to let go. She eventually thought of ringing the dealer who bought some of her furniture to ask if he had seen it but, by then, it was too late; he'd sold it and would not be persuaded to give her the name of the buyer."

"Does she know Trabzon?"

"She went there with my father during a cruise of the Black Sea. It was their last holiday together. That's why I bought the picture. She always calls the place Trebizond, like the Rose Macaulay book."

"I'd be happy to leave the painting with you," he said. "It obviously means a lot to her."

"I think you should give it to her yourself. I'm sure she'd want to thank you in person. When she's back. She had a last-minute opportunity to follow part of the Silk Road with her friend Judith Ottery. Someone had dropped out unexpectedly. When last I heard, they were visiting caravanserais in Bukhara. That's Uzbekistan, I think."

"A far cry from Newton FitzPosset."

"And The Old Rectory. In the meantime, most of her remaining stuff is in storage."

After supper, the girls ran back upstairs while parents moved on to coffee. Hugh wasn't listening to the conversation. His one thought was how to get back on track before they had to leave. The only way was to be direct.

"You said your mother's things were in storage. I just wondered where I'd be meeting her. I'd assumed she was going to be living with you."

"This hasn't been settled. In her mind, anyway. She left Dorset with the idea that she'd buy a small flat somewhere in this area so she could retain her independence and avoid being in the way, as she put it. Hence her frantic downsizing. It's hopelessly unrealistic given the way property prices have gone. There's plenty of space for all her stuff without paying for storage but she seems to think that, once it's in this house, it will be here for good and so will she."

"Won't she have to stay here when she's back from the Silk Road?"

"There's nowhere else but she sees it as a temporary measure – pending what, I've no idea."

"Do the things in storage include a box? Specifically, one that would be opened by this key." He pulled it from a pocket with a flourish and laid it on the table. "I found it down the side of one of the wing chairs your mother sold. It was in the cottage we had in Dorset."

"She didn't say she'd mislaid a key as well as a painting. Have some more coffee while I get the list."

Rachel came back a few minutes later with the inventory of items held at Peace o' Mind Self Storage, together with some photographs in a plastic wallet. She riffled through the list – downsizing notwithstanding, it ran to several pages – and found a reference to: 'Victorian camphor wood box with brass fittings. Locked: contents unexamined.' The corresponding photograph showed a richly coloured box with brass corners, edges and handles and a brass plate in need of a polish. It was less clear how big the thing was; the list gave no dimensions and the photograph had no scale.

"One good turn deserves another," she said. "I'll retrieve the box and we'll take it from there. I don't suppose my mother will mind. If it opens, we've done her a favour, haven't we? Keep the key; I'll only lose it."

"Do the names on the label mean anything to you?" put in Kate.

Rachel picked it up and looked thoughtful. "I don't recognise The Grove," she said, "but I do believe that Lionel Pybus was my great-grandfather. On my mother's side."

Six

Kate told him to be patient when he suggested dropping Rachel a gentle reminder. It had been almost two weeks, he said. Had she forgotten or changed her mind or was she simply waiting until her mother was back? Mrs Badingham's return must surely be imminent. How long had she been away?

And then a message on Saturday morning and a short drive to The Old Rectory. Just him.

"I was waiting for Guy to come with me," said Rachel as she led him to the sitting room. "I wasn't sure how heavy it would be and he's not the easiest person to pin down."

The box gleamed large on the rug in front of the fireplace.

"It's a military campaign chest, according to Guy. It weighs a ton. How far that's the box and how far what's inside, I don't know. I gave it a once-over with beeswax and Brasso. Guy says if it doesn't open we can use it as a coffee table." She was talking too fast, sounded nervous. "I'm not sure what my mother would think of that, but then I'm not sure what she thinks about a lot of things."

"This is the moment of truth," said Hugh, extracting the key and passing it to her. "Short drum roll."

She knelt in front of the box and inserted the key into the lock. It turned part-way but no further.

He joined her in front of the box and jiggled the key. It would move neither forward nor back and resisted his attempts to ease it out of the lock in order to start again.

"Do you have any WD40?"

After several minutes of careful lubrication and gentle coaxing, the key turned home with a satisfying click. They lifted the lid until it was open as far as it would go, held at the horizontal by two solid brass hinges. Kneeling side by side, they stared at the contents of the box, saying nothing at first as they tried to get the measure of the mass of material inside. Hugh was desperate to take a closer look, find out what was there, and sensed that Rachel was as excited as he was. But she looked overwhelmed and he held back, reluctant to start rummaging on his own. He willed her to make a move. They couldn't stop now.

It would be easier and more comfortable, she said, to look at the stuff at the kitchen table. It was there they lugged the box, celebrating their achievement with a glass of wine before setting to. She removed papers and photographs, some loose, many in folders; albums and notebooks; theatre programmes; newspaper cuttings. She surveyed the piles and did no more than nod when he pointed to the small storage section at the side of the box. It had a lid of its own, which he raised to expose a jumble of coins and stamps; bus and train tickets; a grubby white five-pound note, folded in half and half again; an emerald green fountain pen; several pencil stubs and broken blackboard chalks; a seal and a part-used stick of sealing wax.

He picked out the seal and placed it in his palm. The handle looked like agate; the seal itself was probably brass, though so dirty it was hard to be sure. He tilted the seal so that the face was under one of the spots. The image was indistinct. A spiral, he thought at first, or maybe concentric circles, like rings on a target or ripples on a pond.

He passed it to Rachel for a second opinion.

"The image is in reverse," she said. "Intaglio. We need to see it the right way round. We could melt some sealing wax." She reached for the stick of bright red wax in Lionel's box and paused. "Or use some of Willow's modelling clay."

As she headed for the stairs, Hugh turned to the piles on the rest of the table. There was little he could do in the time available. He flicked through a leather-covered album of press cuttings. Several of the cuttings, he noted, had headlines about a fire at a country house, though the building looked intact in the murky photographs that accompanied the reports. The names of the papers concerned were inked untidily on the cuttings, together with a date in November 1902. He wondered how old

Lionel Pybus would have been then and whether the writing was his.

At the sound of footsteps, he quickly closed the album and put it back. Rachel marched in, breathless and with an air of triumph. She held a small wedge of plasticine. She worked it between two hands, flattened it on the table and pressed the seal into the clay.

Set within a square border, four concentric circles. Or almost so, for there appeared to be gaps in some and solid connections between others, with a dot, like a pimple, in the middle of the innermost circle.

"Looks a bit like a labyrinth," said Rachel.

"Or a maze."

"Why use it for a seal? It's pretty cumbersome."

"Your mother may know."

"When she decides to reappear. She should be here by now but she's spending a few days with Judith Ottery." She stared despondently at the piles on the table. "We'll never look through all these papers before Guy gets back with the girls."

"At least we've made some progress. Did you mean to leave that one in the box?"

He was pointing to a foolscap folder lying in the bottom. As she lifted it out, the edges crumbled and it fell open. A single sheet of paper, folded in two, slipped to the table in front of Hugh. He pinched the halves apart and smoothed them flat.

"It's the maze on the seal!" said Rachel.

"It's not quite the same. The circles are surrounded by three squares, making seven walls in all."

"The seal shows the central part of the maze. This is the complete version. It's neatly done. Looks like watercolour and still fresh and bright."

"Almost glowing," said Hugh. "But why is it orange?"

"Why not? It's just a colour."

"No colour is just a colour. You'd expect it to be green, if it's a hedge maze"

"Maybe it's one of those low-level mazes in brick or stone."

"The impression in the clay suggests that the walls are higher, standing proud as if projecting well above the ground."

"Assuming it's a real maze. It could just be an emblem or symbol or logo of some sort."

"Where does Lionel Pybus fit in? There must be some connection; the seal and the plan were in his box."

She shrugged and looked at her watch.

"We'd better put this stuff back. As you say, my mother may have some answers."

"Is there any chance of borrowing the plan so I can look at it at home?"

"How about a photocopy?"

Eleanor and Rosie made short work of finding the way to the centre of the maze. He had taken further copies of the plan and set them the test. They completed it a good deal quicker than he did. Even Kate was drawn in. She suggested a link between the orange on the plan and 'The Grove' on the label of the key. "As in orange grove. In the Mediterranean, for example."

"You may be right. I just assumed The Grove was a house somewhere in England. It's a common enough name so it could be anywhere and I haven't found one that owns up to a maze like this."

"It's a rather yellowy orange, isn't it," said Rosie solemnly, holding a copy directly under the light. "Like the amber of Grandma's brooch."

"I think it's like flames or molten lava," said Eleanor. "A maze on fire!"

Later that evening, he sent an email to Rachel. He mentioned an incident at a country house in 1902, reported in newspaper cuttings he had spotted while she was out of the room.

Seven

*H*ugh followed Beadles Lane until he came to the entrance of Assendene Court. The drive meandered through open parkland, clumps and scatterings of giant oaks set against a distant background of wooded hills. The grounds owed much to a far-sighted landscape gardener in the eighteenth century. His attempts to improve upon nature were not always appreciated in their day. Now they were regarded as providing a perfect setting for the house, which gradually came into view, guarded, as it seemed, by two large cedars at the front.

The house itself was mainly Tudor with alterations and additions over the years. He slowed to admire the gabled façade, banded with brick and flint, shimmering gently in the brilliance of the day. He would happily have lingered longer. But his route took him round to the left, following signs to the staff car park and the service block tucked discreetly out of sight.

Rachel had scanned the newspaper cuttings and sent them to him. The house was in Oxfordshire, the incident a fire that had destroyed a maze over a century ago. The property's website made no mention of the fire but listed among the attractions of the place a maze planted in the 1960s. Assendene Court was not one of the houses in the care of the Heritage Commission but it lay within striking distance of one that was. Hugh found an excuse to visit that house first and see for himself the work of conserving and restoring the Chinese wallpaper recently uncovered there.

This afternoon he had an appointment with Simon Marmion, previously an assistant manager at Brockley House in Hampshire (where Hugh had first met him) and now house manager at Assendene Court. Simon had suggested a Monday as the house (though not the park) was closed to the public and he could give Hugh his more-or-less undivided attention. He had promised to do a little research beforehand.

Simon wheezed down the passage to his office and squashed into the chair at his desk, sweating and breathing heavily in the unseasonable warmth. Hugh was taken aback by the change in his appearance since Brockley days. He could scarcely have been described as slight even then; now he was obese.

After a minute or two, Simon invited him to pull up a chair of his own and look at the sepia photographs lying on the table next to the desk. They showed the original maze, before and after the fire, some taken from the gardens, others giving a bird's-eye view from the upper floors of the house. The destruction was near-total.

"It's one thing for a fire to cause damage," said Hugh, "but I can't see how it would destroy a maze of this size completely."

"This all happened in Sir Ralph Assendene's day, long before the advent of the trust that runs the place now. Fire-fighting facilities on-site were limited by all accounts and it took the local men a long time to arrive."

"They had garden hoses, surely, even then?"

"They did but their deployment, it appears, was a little slow and mainly confined to damping down at the end."

"How did the fire start?"

"The official version was that the gardener's boy was burning dry leaves too enthusiastically and too close to the maze, which caught alight. The maze was beech rather than yew in those days. It would have been dry itself at that time of year; the paths in the maze were narrow so the hedges were close together, enabling the flames to spread quickly."

"And unofficially?"

Simon leaned forward a little and lowered his voice. "That the gardener's boy had nothing to do with it and the fire was started deliberately – and not at a single point. There are hints in the archives that it could have been an act of arson by a member of the family or someone staying with them." He sat back, raised his hands and shrugged. "Nothing, it seems, was proved."

"Why would anyone want to destroy a maze? It must have taken some planning."

"A dare, perhaps. Or revenge. Possibly for something that happened in the maze itself."

"Even so. Why was the maze not replaced for sixty years?"

"There were attempts to install box hedges on the same pattern but they were not successful. The hedges were grubbed up and the area fell into disuse, as did large parts of the garden during and between the wars. Eventually, the family gave up the struggle and sold the place to the actor Clive Paragon. He and his wife set about refurbishing the property, inside and out."

"Although the maze was not replanted in beech."

"The Paragons took the view that beech hedges look dead in winter, become tatty and unsightly, and lose all sense of mystery because you can see through the walls. Yew hedges overcame these objections, though they're a devil to maintain."

"A popular attraction these days, according to your website."

"Strictly from the outside; the maze has been closed to the public since 2002. Health and safety."

They took the service lift to the second floor. From rear bedroom windows, they looked over the maze, bathed in sunlight, the walled garden beyond. At this height, the maze made sense; it had a satisfying symmetry and shape when seen as a whole. But it was also unsettling, as if the seal had grown to enormous dimensions and come to life in the centre of the enclosing squares.

Simon was keen to return to the lift. As Hugh took

a last look through the windows he was struck by the thought that they offered not merely an overview of the maze but an opportunity to spy on people using it, to take pleasure in the frantic attempts of anyone lost to find a way out. Before the maze was closed, at any rate.

Simon dropped to his desk for a breather, as he put it, while Hugh brought water from the cooler in the passage. The heat was becoming oppressive. When his host was ready, Hugh swirled his jacket over the back of a chair and followed him through dim corridors to a door opening on to the terrace and the dazzle that lay outside. They trudged down steps and across close-cut grass until Simon stopped at a pavilion in the shade of a large Spanish chestnut. It was a hexagonal brick-built structure with a shingle roof erected in the early nineteenth century as a place of rest and relaxation. Nowadays it was used as a space for information and exhibits about the house and its history. But this was not why Simon had brought him.

Inside, a stained-glass window, hit by the full force of the afternoon sun, drenched the pavilion with orange light. As his eyes adjusted, Hugh could make out the burning image of the maze, projected on to the floor and the opposite wall. The glass itself glowed like amber, as Rosie had said about the plan. He wondered which came first: the plan or the seal or the window and what the relationship between them might be.

"Of course, it's more recent than the pavilion," said Simon. "The gift of an anonymous donor. The maze was something of a motif in this place. Elizabeth Mayes was an ancestor of the Assendenes. One of them thought it amusing to adopt the maze symbol as a mark of their heritage. It crops up on notepaper, bookplates, crockery from the late 1800s on. Planting the original beech maze was all part of it. Now we use the maze symbol on mugs, mouse mats, tea towels, and the like. They're very popular with the visitors."

"I must pay a visit to the shop before I go," said Hugh, "but, tell me, does the name Lionel Pybus ring any bells? He seems to have had a connection with the house but I don't know what or when."

Simon shook his head and said he would speak to the archivist in the morning. A chirrup from his phone distracted him and reminded Hugh that his own phone was in the jacket in the manager's office, despite Kate's instruction to keep the thing with him.

"Sorry," said Simon. "I need to deal with this. I'll be back in a jiff."

Hugh watched the lumbering form recede and turned to the leaflets and display boards. These began to pall after a while. There was no sign of Simon or means of contacting him, short of going back to the house or finding a member of staff. He picked up a map of the grounds. The pavilion was some distance from the shop and café but not so far from the maze. He wrote a note on a form intended for visitor comments, using one of the pencils provided, and pulled the door behind him.

The sun was slipping but the day was still pleasantly

warm as he pushed past the barrier and approached the entrance of the maze. It was flanked by limestone columns topped by balls bearing the masks of tragedy and comedy. An allusion, perhaps, to Clive Paragon's career on the stage, now largely forgotten.

As he took his first faltering steps into the maze, he was struck by the height of the hedges, eight feet at least, soaring above him. And by how thick they were, how solid and confining, how narrow the path between them. He turned the first corner and felt for the plan of the maze he had brought to Assendene, the one on which Rosie and Eleanor had marked the route to the centre and how to get out again. Damn. It was in his jacket with the phone.

Never mind. How long should he allow to do the maze? Twenty minutes? Half an hour? That should be plenty. And hadn't he read somewhere that by following the outside walls of a maze consistently to the left he would arrive back at the entrance? Or was it the right? Or was that a different sort of maze entirely? He found himself walking faster but the sense of progress was illusory as he came to a dead-end, turned back and wondered which way he had come and which way he should go. He could have done with a ball of thread.

He stumbled further into the maze and further from the entrance and the outside world. He was becoming disoriented, his decisions increasingly arbitrary when faced with choices. Had he been along here before? It all looked the same. The walls seemed even taller, the sharp, straight sides tighter and more impenetrable. And the silence was absolute. The bird song had tailed away. He could hear nothing; and no one, he realised, could hear him. Had Simon found his note? Would someone come looking?

It was cold. The light was fading, the walls becoming darker. He found it hard to see as he blundered forward, the panic rising. And the anger too: the situation was absurd. He could only be yards from the way he had come in. How long had he been here? He could not even read his watch.

The silence was broken by an insistent rustling from under a hedge. And then a slithering, but whether coming closer or moving away he could not tell. A sudden scream. A fox? An owl? He started to run, his mouth and throat dry. He grasped that he had left behind the squares of the outer section of the maze and was following, in fits and starts, circles that were getting smaller. At length, he fell into an open area. It was lighter here than in the body of the maze. He made out, ghostly white against the darkness of the hedge opposite, a long stone bench. He dropped to it and, arms folded, breathing heavily, he leaned forward and stared at the pitted paving in front of him. He was exhausted.

After a few minutes, he eased himself up and over to the statue on the plinth at the centre. Encrusted with lichen, a representation of Pan, horned and hoofed, leering malevolently as he gripped his pipe. Beneath, carved in relief on the front of the plinth, the maze in miniature, as if to taunt those who had struggled to reach their goal – or to celebrate their success. But

Hugh's only thought was how to escape from the maze and get back to the house.

Nothing would induce him to return by those dizzying paths through the blackness of the interior. Nor could he stay here. And then he remembered that the maze had a separate exit. The dark circle surrounding him appeared unbroken; he could not even see how he had entered it. He followed the hedge round until he spotted a pale sign, framed by yew, that must have been left after public closure of the maze. It was in the shape of a pointing hand: WAY OUT.

He burst from the exit as if propelled by an unseen force. He came to a halt on an area of grass and steadied himself on the edge of a marble urn. It was smooth and unexpectedly warm to the touch. How long had he been in that place? One hour, two? He tilted the face of his watch to catch the sunset stretched between the trees in the distance. Barely three-quarters of an hour.

He found himself among topiary. Clipped cones and balls and cubes of yew, a pair of disdainful peacocks, and a pig, glum and unresponsive in the gathering dusk. A crunch of gravel, a rumble of wheels, as a gardener, emerging from the walled garden, trundled a handcart along a path and vanished in the gloom. Hugh could see the back of the house now; taking the terrace steps two at a time he made for the door he thought he had been through earlier with Simon. It was locked. There was no bell and he doubted that rapping would be heard in the service wing. As he passed the front of the house, en route to the side entrance he had used when he first arrived, he saw the headlights of cars moving slowly towards Beadles Lane. The house itself was in darkness.

The side door was pulled sharply inwards just as he reached for the handle. He came face to face with the shop manager, Pamela Quince, who yelped and flattened against the wall of the corridor. Hugh stuttered why he was there and they went together to the manager's office. On the desk, a carrier bag for him, she said, with some souvenirs Simon had asked her to put together. Of the manager himself there was no sign.

He lifted his jacket from the back of a chair and slipped it on, feeling in a pocket for his phone. He ought to let Kate know he would be back later than expected. But first he said,

"Where is Simon likely to be if he's not here?"

They found him in the library, slumped at a desk with a leather-bound volume, the boards embossed in gilt with the emblem of a maze. A heart attack, the paramedics said; he must have died almost immediately.

Hugh felt weak, unsteady. It was hard to take in; he had been talking to Simon barely more than an hour ago, toured the house and grounds with him, felt the force of the amber glow in the pavilion. He stayed until the ambulance had left and Pamela had locked the place and set the alarm. Then he located his car and prepared to make a call.

Eight

I think I should warn you," said Rachel as they loitered in the hall of The Old Rectory, "she's taken to wearing items of Uzbek dress. Not all the time, of course. Only when it's likely to cause embarrassment or inconvenience to others. Mostly to me."

Hugh suppressed a smile and muttered a platitude. He was already feeling apprehensive about the encounter, wondering how it would go. How much did she know and how much would she tell him on a first meeting? Lionel, Assendene, the maze in the seal, the one that burnt down, the stained-glass window in the pavilion, the watercolour at the bottom of the box. He would have to play it by ear.

"A purple skull cap in the local supermarket. Can you imagine? Embroidered in gold. And matching slippers with pointed toes. They seemed to find it amusing at the checkout. The children only encourage her and Guy sniggers behind his newspaper. I'm surprised she hasn't pitched a yurt in the back garden. Or even the front, knowing her."

They took a few steps towards the sitting room and Rachel stopped again. She went all confidential and said,

"We had some friends round last night. My mother stood on a coffee table and recited the whole of *The Golden Journey to Samarkand*. When she'd finished she insisted we all drink a toast to Flecker. I can't think what they made of her in Dorset."

"Ah. Mr Mullion. The great detective. We meet at last. I'm sorry I've been so elusive. I was detained in Chalfont St Giles with my friend Judith Ottery. She caught the dreaded lurgy while we were away and needed someone with her. I blame the *plov* she had in Bukhara. Do you know the 'Stans?"

Hester Badingham was smaller than he had expected, almost elfin, with mouse-gold hair and the suspicion of a tan. She must, he thought, be well into her seventies but she had a younger air and a mischievous twinkle in her eye. He could tell straightaway they would get on.

As to her dress, it looked pretty conventional. Apart from the silk pantaloons: jagged chevrons of black and lemon yellow, magenta and turquoise, topped with a wide floral waistband. They shimmered in the light of a standard lamp as if they had life and movement of their own. The effect was disconcerting.

Rachel brought in some tea, glanced at the pantaloons, and left them to it. The preliminaries over, Hugh reached for his bag and pulled out a picture. He unwound the bubble wrap and passed the painting to her.

"*Market in Trabzon*," he said. "Returned to its rightful owner."

"Thank you. And for all your trouble. This picture means a lot to me." She dabbed her eyes with a handkerchief pulled quietly from her sleeve. "The antique dealer's men took the wrong one. They were supposed to remove a ghastly Landseer print my late husband won in a raffle. Hardly an antique but Nigel Gosling offered to take it. Why he refused to give me the name of the woman who bought my picture I don't know. It can't have meant much to her if she gave it away. Though I suppose I'm lucky she did."

"And it helped to track down the previous owner of the chairs and reunite the key with the box."

"Ah yes, the box."

Rachel had said on the phone that her mother had spent hours alone in her room looking through the box. "It seems to have affected her but she won't say why."

"I've had it for fifty years," said Hester. "Ever since he died. In fact, a little earlier. He wanted me to take it 'before the vultures descended'. That's how he put it. He wasn't worried about anything else."

"Would that be Lionel Pybus? His name is on the label. I'm afraid we tore it when retrieving the key."

"That's right," she said, waving a hand to dismiss his concern about the label. "'Lionel Pybus, His Box, The Grove'. He was my grandfather and it was indeed his box."

"And The Grove?"

"The name of the boarding house at his prep school:

Broomwood Lodge. On the Kent coast. Queen Victoria was still on the throne when he first went there. Seems incredible, doesn't it? Cold showers and Greek unseens. Staffed by veterans of the Sudan and young men without hope of employment elsewhere. The place closed some years ago. Turned into flats, I shouldn't wonder. I'm surprised it lasted as long as it did."

"Sounds as though you were close to your grandfather."

"We had a similar approach to life. Not too serious. Or so it seemed at the time. He found my mother a bit earnest and disapproving; Rachel takes after her in some ways. He was quite lonely after my grandmother died and was glad to have someone to talk to."

"You could only have been in your…"

"Early twenties. This was towards the end of the 1960s. I had a bedsit in Paddington, he had a terraced house in Camden Town. One of those early nineteenth-century brick and stucco jobs with railings and wrought-iron balconies. Very desirable now but most of the street was seedy and neglected then. The area still had a feel of Sickert about it: he'd only lived down the road in Mornington Crescent.

"It was a big house for one person: three storeys plus basement and dormers. Still had all the original plasterwork. And fireplaces too, not that he would ever use them. He insisted on hideous paraffin heaters all over the place and sent me out to buy the Esso Blue.

"The house was full of furniture and books and pictures, many he'd painted himself."

Hugh sat up, his interest piqued further as a collector of pictures when time and funds allowed.

"He was an artist?"

"He taught at an art school before and after the war and painted in his spare time. Sold a few but he didn't do it for the money; he'd had the sense to marry a woman of means. They moved to the Camden house when he retired. He set up a studio on the first floor and got his paints and brushes from Roberson's around the corner in Parkway. His output increased for a while. Large abstracts, mostly, but I have a few smaller ones that he gave me."

"Do you have them here?"

"They're still in storage." She shifted in her chair and stared at the cup of tea that she had not touched. "Would you pass me my bag?"

She unzipped a pocket at the back and took out a small red leather photograph holder, a double one of the sort that folds like a book. She opened it and he saw two photographs of a man. Recognisably the same man, though taken many years apart. One showed him as he was before the First World War, Hugh guessed, judging by the style of the jacket and the rounded collars of his shirt; the other as an elderly man in a dark three-piece suit, standing in a restaurant or café, upright but relaxed, with the nose and eyes Hugh could see now.

"My grandfather, Lionel Pybus. I took that one after lunch in a Greek place in Pratt Street. We bought some olives on the way back."

It went quiet for a while. Then Hugh, feeling at a

loss, said, "He looks a kindly man."

"He was always good to me. He suggested several times that I move in with him. There was plenty of space."

"But you stayed put in Paddington?"

"I did for a while and then I moved on. Subsisting with the help of Katherine Whitehorn, as we all did. *Cooking in a Bedsitter.* I believe it's still in print. Very much 'cooking to stay alive' rather than 'cooking to impress', in my case. I used to swear by her Turbigo Kidneys.

"I've always valued my independence and, in those days, there were other irons in the fire, so to speak. But I went to see my grandfather as often as I could, took him flowers from Inverness Street market. And once a chamber pot with a face painted inside. He put a maidenhair fern in it. It didn't last, but what does?"

She was beginning to look tired, he thought. Time for a change of tack.

"Did you know the Johnsons when you were in Dorset? Dorothy and George; they lived in Newton FitzPosset for many years."

"Good heavens, yes," she said. "They were friends of ours. Some people found Dorothy a bit difficult; I always thought of her as a kindred spirit." The glint in her eye had returned. "But how do you know them?" She paused for a moment, then said, "You're not *that* Hugh, are you? The one who found the book?"

He nodded and tried to look modest. The book was the second volume of *The Portrait of a Lady*, with

Dorothy's ownership signature on the flyleaf and a note hidden inside. He reunited it with volume I and learned a lot more about Dorothy than he had expected.

"How extraordinary. She was rather impressed by your sleuthing. I do believe we must have met before – or, at least, been in the same place at the same time. At Dorothy's funeral. We were away for George's."

As he was preparing to go, he retrieved a postcard from his bag and gave it to her.

"I picked this up at Assendene," he said. "It's a view of the maze as it was in about 1900. I'm guessing your grandfather may have known it."

Her eyes narrowed and she said quietly,

"Perhaps we should have another chat."

There was an edge to her voice that had not been there before.

Nine

*T*heir birthdays were a few days apart, Kate and Sue. While Kate viewed her approaching fortieth with equanimity, Sue felt no reason to celebrate her own. Thus the occasion, a small dinner party at number twelve Falstaff Road, was rebranded a welcome home party for Sue. They bought her a present anyway.

They had known her for the best part of fifteen years and had missed her while she was away teaching in Italy. The house was quieter without her visits, even with Eleanor and Rosie on the loose.

"It's Mullion of the Yard," she squealed, as Hugh came into the sitting room from saying goodnight to the twins. She put down her glass of wine, ran towards him and gave him a hug. She seemed just the same, her short blonde hair that looked bleached but wasn't. "I hear you're up to your old tricks. Books last time, now pictures and keys."

"Ten years apart. Hardly excessive."

"First he creates a mystery," put in Kate, "then he becomes obsessed with trying to solve it. I don't know why he can't leave things alone." Perhaps she had forgotten that *she* had retrieved the missing half of the label that completed Lionel's name and arranged the first contact with Rachel – and identified what was written on the note he discovered inside the book all those years ago. The exasperation she sometimes felt was tempered by an amused tolerance extending to moral and practical support and even interest in the outcome of his detective work.

"I don't like loose ends," said Hugh. "Anyway, you can blame *him* for the book. I found it in a box outside his shop."

He was pointing to Anthony Buffo, owner of Toad Books, a tall man with a small black moustache and faintly olive skin. Anthony wasn't listening. He was studying the coaster from which he had lifted his glass. He looked quizzical.

"It's ringing a bell," he said. "The maze motif; I've seen it before."

"The coasters came from Assendene Court. It's a country house in Oxfordshire. The family that used to live there adopted it as a badge or symbol on things like crockery and bookplates."

They adjourned to the dining room and conversation turned to other matters. Then, as Anthony passed the cheese to Sue, he said,

"That's it! It's coming back to me. A collection of books I bought a few weeks ago. One of them had the maze mark; not as a bookplate but on the cover. I only took them because the man said he knew me from the old days in South Kensington when I ran the Romulus Gallery. He had a brick-red face and trousers to match. I didn't remember him at all."

Kate looked up when Hugh asked if he could see the books.

"Don't forget the Rule," she said.

She was referring to the Roberts Rule, which she had introduced (when Roberts was still her surname) in a forlorn attempt to control the rising tide of books, initially at the old house in Dogberry Road. It was located tantalisingly close to Toad Books. Put simply, the Rule required any acquisition to be balanced by a disposal. Books for the twins were exempt on educational grounds and the Rule had never applied to her own. Hugh became adept at smuggling.

"As if I would," he said. And then to Anthony, "Have you ever come across an artist called Lionel Pybus? He died in the late 1960s, I think, so well before you had the Romulus Gallery. Painted abstracts; towards the end of his life, at least."

Anthony shook his head and reached for his glass.

"I'll see if I can find anything."

Hugh parked in Costard Street and walked round the corner to the parade. Toad Books – second-hand and antiquarian books bought and sold; collections purchased – was roughly in the middle, flanked by a betting shop and the bakery he still thought of as new. In fact, several years had passed since it had taken over the premises of the off-licence he used to visit on his way back from the station in Dogberry Road days. The bookshop itself was unchanged, apart from the window display which this month featured a display of film and theatre books, backed by posters and handbills of West End productions from the 1950s.

He hovered over the boxes outside, may even have dipped into the one that had previously contained bananas, but remembered why he was here and pushed into the shop. It was as warm and welcoming as ever and smelled of freshly brewed coffee. To the right was the gallery area, a bright white room in which a few people were circulating, holding cups and looking at pictures. He went to the left and the mousy woman at the cash desk. She was hard at work on her Sudoku.

"Good morning, Marjorie."

"Mr Mullet! You did give me a fright. We haven't seen you in a while. How are Kate and the girls?"

Before he could reply, a piercing whistle split the air. It came from the African grey parrot sitting on top of its cage near the window.

"Good morning, Charlie. Is all well with the world?"

"Bugger off," said the parrot, turning to face away.

"Charlie, you're a bad bird," said Marjorie. "He's been in a difficult mood since Mr Buffo ran out of corks."

"I brought some with me," he said, pulling a polythene bag from his jacket pocket. "I'll give them to Anthony. Where is he, by the way? He's got some books for me to look at."

★

He climbed the stairs to the first floor and edged past piles of boxes lining the corridor on both sides. He was making for the door at the end. Marjorie, he reflected, must now be much the same age as Hester Badingham. Happily, she had never taken to wearing pantaloons. She had been with the shop from the start and showed no sign of retiring, not that her duties were unduly onerous. He had given up reminding her that his surname was Mullion or suggesting that she call him 'Hugh'.

As he raised a hand to knock, the door was pulled open to frame Anthony in the entrance to his office. He started when he saw Hugh and retreated into the room, accepting the bag of corks presented to him like an offering. He waved Hugh towards a chair and bent to retrieve, from the other side of his desk, a large carrier bag bearing the name of a Jermyn Street tailor.

"I've not had time to go through them properly. Some, the man said, came from his London flat, others from his cottage in Dorset, though which books came from which property I've no idea."

He removed the books in batches and piled them on the documents already covering the desk. Many were paperbacks of the thriller and adventure kind. They were interspersed with an apparently random selection of cookery and travel books and hardback novels issued by a book club that had been defunct for many years. Then, from under a work on flower arranging, he produced a slim volume bound in burgundy leather. The spine was blank but the front cover had the emblem of a maze tooled in gold. It gleamed in the sharp light of the desk lamp.

Hugh reached over to take it, heart pounding. The symbol on the cover was identical to the ones he had seen before. The volume itself comprised plain pages of the palest cream. Plain in that there was no printing; it was not a book as such but more of a diary or journal, the pages covered in notes and drawings. None of the entries was dated, as far as he could see.

The drawings included versions of the maze symbol: some crude, even frantic, others more refined. Or perhaps they were sketches of the maze at Assendene itself, before it was destroyed by fire. And then, towards the end, some that seemed to show hedges ablaze, a conflagration, in which a statue of Pan in the middle remained untouched.

How did the volume end up here? The man with the brick-red trousers who had sold the books to Anthony must surely have been the disagreeable man he had met at January Cottage in Newton FitzPosset. Hester was, after all, the previous occupier and she had some sort of Assendene connection through her grandfather. But how could she have left this one behind? Even if it was mislaid in the chaos of the move, would she not have noticed by now and tried to get it back? Perhaps not; most of her stuff was in storage and she may have assumed it was with them. If she had thought about it at all. Whatever the explanation, the volume had been well looked after. Its condition was pristine.

The only point on which he was clear was that he

couldn't study the volume with the care required and absorb the details while he was sitting in Anthony's office. Anthony said he could keep it and would accept no money on condition that he maintained a supply of corks for Charlie.

"Let me know if you discover anything of interest. By the way, I had a word with Neville Pink, the pictures man at Gavels. Seems they've auctioned several paintings by your Lionel Pybus over the years. Well regarded by a discerning few, was how he put it. Not prolific, if the market is anything to go by, but persistent. Late Pybus is rather different in style from the early efforts, apparently. He suggested that you look at the archive on Gavels' website and take it from there."

Ten

*H*ugh had the house to himself. Kate had taken the girls to buy ballet shoes at a shop in St Martin's Lane before going on to explore Covent Garden. That should give him a few hours.

He bounded up the stairs to his study two at a time. He removed from the bottom drawer of the filing cabinet the volume Anthony had given him and took it over to his desk. Despite his conviction that it must have belonged at some stage to Lionel Pybus there was nothing, on the face of it, to indicate that Lionel was responsible for the contents or that he had owned the thing at all.

Flicking through the notes and sketches Hugh dislodged a card that had been inserted between two blank pages towards the end. It was a dinner menu, dated 25th March 1902, from the Grand Oriental Hotel in Colombo. It listed a formidable number of courses, including, he noticed, a savoury in the form of cheese custard. Why was the menu here? Had Lionel been to Ceylon? He could only have been a boy in 1902, presumably still at the prep school in Kent that Hester had mentioned: Broomwood Lodge.

Hugh worked his way through the volume and tried to piece the fragments together. It became clear that this was the work of a young visitor to Assendene Court in the early years of the last century. A school friend of Freddy Assendene, invited to stay for half-term in bleak November. Several comments suggested that he felt out of place in the country house world, though he seems to have been made welcome and coped well enough, at least at first. And a note, matter-of-fact, uncomplaining, that he had overheard a giggling parlour maid refer to their guest as 'Master Lionel Piecrust'. *I have been called worse.*

This surely confirmed it. These were the thoughts and impressions of Lionel Pybus. He did indeed have a connection with Assendene, though poor Simon Marmion had not recognised the name that day and had never had the chance to pursue it with the archivist.

Lionel had been given a bedroom in the family wing, normally reserved for visiting cousins and Lady Assendene's unmarried sister, Violet, on rare trips home from her villa in Menton. This may have accounted for the eclectic mix of reading matter he found in the room, ranging from works by Henty and Mrs Molesworth and the Fairy Books of Andrew Lang, to Trollope's Barchester novels, several by Conrad and Jane Austen, a random Maria Corelli and books of poetry in English and French. These were joined by copies of

Country Life that had made their way from the table in the drawing room.

I read some of the poems in The Oxford Book of English Verse *before putting out the light. I liked them well enough. Freddy says that poetry is for girls but all the poems I looked at are by men and mostly ones we had already read at school.*

Lionel had found the blank journal in a drawer in his room. *Freddy said I could use it* 'for jottings and whatnot' *but it was Isabel who brought me ink and blotting paper from the school room. She said it was easy as the governess was away visiting her family. I had pencils and my Parker fountain pen, though filling it was very messy. Isabel asked if I would like to draw a likeness of her. I said I would.*

Isabel, Hugh concluded, was Freddy Assendene's younger sister. The journal contained many drawings of a girl, presumably her, mostly in pencil, mostly drawn on separate sheets – Assendene notepaper, by the look of it – and stuck in later. The last one was different. Perhaps the same girl, perhaps not. It was done in ink directly on the page; underneath, the words '*From memory*'.

Lionel said a bit about his bedroom at Assendene, half-panelled with flowered wallpaper above. It was the pictures that had made an impression: watercolours in identical gilt frames: scenes of the Italian lakes, Rome, Venice. They were the work of Lady Assendene and there were others by her in the morning room. *Freddy's mother showed an interest in my drawing and asked if she might have a portrait of Isabel. I went to my room to fetch one for her and met the housemaid who had come to draw the curtains and light the fire. Her name was Sarah. She said she hoped I would come back as Master Freddy's other friends hardly ever did. I said I hoped so too. Lady Assendene said she was pleased with my drawing and asked me what I thought of the pictures in the house. I said that Gainsborough and Sir Thomas Lawrence were fine painters but I preferred the ones by her. When she laughed she looked like Isabel.*

Lionel spoke of the views, from the window of his room, over parkland to the rear of the house, of the beech woods on distant hills, and of the maze closer to hand. Hugh wondered if he had been in that room himself when he was at Assendene. The bedrooms now were largely empty and off the route the public took.

The days after Lionel's arrival were evidently grey and damp and the children confined to the house with such forgotten distractions as hunt the whistle, dumb crambo and hot cockles (*Freddy made my hand smart very much.*). A session of old maid degenerated when Isabel was left with the last card, the Queen of Spades. *Freddy said that meant she would be an old maid herself. Isabel burst into tears and ran to her room. I thought I had better stay where I was.*

Charades after five o'clock tea one day resulted in a rare sighting of Sir Ralph Assendene, back from a board meeting in London. No doubt, thought Hugh, he had collected a few undemanding directorships in exchange for the Assendene name to supplement his income from farm rents. Afterwards (*I was required to act 'artichoke' and 'earwig'.*) Sir Ralph showed Lionel his Game Book. *It was bound in black leather and had lists of animals and birds that had been shot. They were mostly pheasants but there were hares and rabbits and woodcock and other things too. I asked why it was necessary to kill so many but Freddy said that was the point and his father said I would come to know country ways. I don't think I shall.*

The November weather improved, with extended periods of blue sky and sunshine. The children were let loose in the grounds, running around the lake and through the woods, poking into glasshouses, and generally getting in the way of the gardeners. It was Freddy who led them into the maze and took them to the centre. The beech hedges were thinning and no longer green. *I told Freddy that, in the sun, the maze looked more orange than brown, like the marmalade we had at breakfast. Isabel said it was like amber and we should call it 'The Amber Maze' but Freddy just pinched her and told her not to be an idiot. He did not explain what he meant and Isabel was quiet. I did not say that, from my window, I could see the maze and had spotted him going in and coming out at times we were supposed to be indoors. He had been carrying a sack.*

The journal had sketches of the maze as seen from Lionel's window and from ground level, the entrance flanked by different statues from the ones in place when Hugh was there. Next to the sketches, reproductions of the maze symbol, echoing the one on the cover, the drawings neat at first, then progressively looser, wilder.

After breakfast, Freddy took me along the lake path to the boat house. The rowing boat and punts were already drawn inside for the winter. I could hear the ducks quacking on the water. They were mallards like the ones we have on the pond in our local park. Freddy said it was time for me to join his secret society and that all the boys from school who had visited Assendene had joined as well. I asked if Isabel was a member but he said she was not eligible as she was a girl. When I asked what the society was for, he said that it was to be ready when the time came and that I would know when it did. It could be soon or many years away. A test would be involved; it would take place that afternoon. He did not ask me if I wanted to be a member.

He told me to stand by the statue of Pan at the centre of the maze and not to move until he came back. The exit would be closed, though he did not say why. Then he left me.

I heard the crackle and the hissing before I saw that the hedges were on fire. In the breeze that had got up the flames spread quickly. The smoke made it difficult to breath and it was very hot. I wanted to run. I remembered what Freddy had said but the hedge by the exit was on fire too so I do not know how he could have come back. Or where I could have run. I was surrounded by flames, in the middle of a circle of fire. I heard shouts. Two of the gardeners rushed in by the exit path. They were wearing caps and gloves, scarves to their faces, holding sheets of canvas to shield them from the burning as best they could. They pulled me away from the statue and took me out like a bundle. Lady Assendene and Isabel were waiting on the grass. They seemed relieved that I was not harmed. I went with them to the house.

From my window, I saw the smoking ruins of the maze. The fire engine had been late in arriving and slow to pump water from the lake. The men put out the last of the flames but could do nothing to save the hedges. Lady Assendene said she had telegraphed my aunt about the 'dreadful accident', as she called it, but Sarah told me later that Freddy had dipped rags in lamp oil stolen from the housekeeper's store and set them alight. I do not know how she knows and I have not seen Freddy since he left me by the statue of Pan. It is still standing.

I said goodbye to Isabel in the hall. She made me promise that I would see her again but I have no idea when. Lady Assendene came with me to the station in the new Daimler. As we were leaving the grounds, I looked up at the rooks in the high elms near the lodge. They were as noisy as they had been when I arrived. I saw pheasants feeding on stubble in the fields we passed along Beadles Lane and wondered how long they would survive. I had heard there was to be another shooting party at the end of the month.

At the station, Lady Assendene gave me a bag of cakes that cook had made and an envelope. She said I should open it on the train. As it puffed out, I caught sight of her sitting in the car. She turned away when she saw me. She looked upset. I ate one of the cakes and opened the envelope. I took out a piece of paper, stiff as a collar and a little larger than a postcard. It was a watercolour of the lake at Assendene in summer. With it was a note with some words said to be from Hazlitt's Table-Talk: 'There is pleasure in painting which none but painters know.'

That was the last entry. The remaining pages were blank, apart from the one with the ink drawing and the words '*From memory*'. The writing of those two words looked older, the letters more confidently formed, than the entries in the rest of the journal. A later addition, perhaps, but there was no indication of timing or its relationship to the rest.

The document was a curiosity. The tone and style of the entries suggested that some were written while he was at Assendene, others after his departure. A record, of sorts, of a brief stay and one that was evidently briefer than originally intended. How old had he been? Did he ever go back? It seemed unlikely.

Lionel came across as a sensitive child rather than the Edwardian ideal of 'the manly boy', preferring poetry and painting to country sports. Hugh imagined him sitting quietly in a Norfolk jacket bought specially for the visit. Yet his apparent passivity was probably no more than a reflection of discomfort in unfamiliar surroundings, a large country house very different, Hugh guessed, from the sort of place Lionel lived, even if he and Freddy went to the same school. Where *did* he live? There was no clue, but not so far from Assendene that a bag of cakes would not tide him over. Or perhaps he was being met en route. And another thing. Lady Assendene had telegraphed his aunt. There was no mention of parents – or brothers and sisters, come to that. Was he an only child, an orphan?

Hugh wondered why Lionel had been invited in the first place. He and Freddy did not seem to have much in common. There was little sense of warmth or friendship between them. Maybe this was less obvious at school, thrown into sharper relief when one of them was on home ground. None of which explained the fire. A disturbing episode, all the more so for the apparent lack of fuss or complaint about an incident that could so easily have resulted in Lionel's death.

The fire was clearly deliberate. What was not clear was whether it was intended to give Lionel a fright, and got out of control, or was designed to destroy the maze and him with it. So much for a membership test for Freddy's 'secret society'. What secret society? Did it exist or was the so-called test an excuse to torment Lionel? Or worse. Other boys were said to have joined but this may not have been true. And if they really had been set tests, these did not involve setting fire to the maze.

Of Freddy, the journal was silent after he left Lionel standing by the statue. He was conspicuous by his absence in the time remaining before Lionel departed for the station. Simon Marmion had said that, in the official version of events, the gardener's boy was blamed for the fire through burning leaves too close to the maze. Unofficially, there was no doubt about the culprit but it was unclear whether he got away scot free or felt the end of his father's horse whip in one of the tack rooms off the stable yard. Either way, after what had happened, he could surely not have returned to face Lionel at Broomwood Lodge.

Hugh felt drained. So many blanks, so many questions. Did it matter after all this time? Everyone involved was long dead. They were no part of *his* family history in any case. But the not-knowing was so frustrating and he was convinced there was something else about Lionel's past, something more he needed to find out. He recalled that he had felt straightaway that the key he had discovered down the side of the chair was the key to more than a box. Perhaps answers lay buried in the box itself or in Hester's memory of things her grandfather had told her. The two were obviously close. Should he remind her that she had suggested another word? The revelation that Lionel was an artist gave an added dimension to the affair.

He settled back to his desk with a mug of tea. As he did so, his foot struck something that yielded softly with a muted rustle. He bent and retrieved from under the desk the carrier bag he had been given that day at Assendene. Having removed some while ago the postcards, coasters, tea towel and the mug he was now using, he had forgotten that the guide to Assendene Court was still in the bag. He had done no more than skim the text and look at a few pictures, intending to go through it properly some other time. He fished out the guide, a slim and glossy A4 booklet with a painting of the house in 1760 reproduced on the front cover. The inevitable maze symbol had been relegated discreetly to the back.

He turned to the section giving an account of the house and its occupants from 1880 to 1939. An uncredited oil portrait of Sir Ralph Assendene showed the young baronet looking proprietorial, if a little nervous, against a sombre background. On the next page, two photographs side-by-side, their subjects in half-profile, taken, he supposed, twenty years or so later. One showed Sir Ralph, the confident country landowner, a moustache spreading beneath his aquiline nose. The other, Lady Assendene, relaxed, delicate-featured, eyes intelligent and good-humoured. Not so different from the final drawing in Lionel's journal but perhaps that was just a case of family resemblance.

The accompanying text was relatively sparse. A bit on Sir Ralph's sporting prowess and his efforts to keep the estate going, largely successfully until the First World War. And then two tragedies. His son Freddy, groomed to succeed him, had been killed at Verdun, and his wife, Olivia, had succumbed to influenza after a trip to London in 1918. She and Freddy were buried in the family crypt in the church of St Mark's, Assendene. There they were joined in 1939 by Sir Ralph himself. The estate passed to his other son, Giles.

Other son? Hugh turned to the family tree at the back. There he was, born in 1912, the third of three children. Neither Giles nor Freddy were married, unlike their sister, Isabel. She was married in 1920 to one Lionel Pybus.

Eleven

*L*ionel married into the Assendenes! Hugh hadn't seen that coming. He wondered what Sir Ralph had thought about it. After the loss of her mother and elder brother, he may not have begrudged Isabel the chance of some happiness. He had soldiered on until the year another war broke out. Isabel, and Lionel with her, must have been back to Assendene many times in the intervening years and presumably while Giles was struggling to keep the place going after his father died. It was not sold to that actor, Clive Paragon, until the 1960s. Odd, therefore, that Simon Marmion had not recognised Lionel's name. Hugh was beginning to wonder whether he should contact the archivist himself.

The family tree in the back of the guide book did not record the names of any children for Lionel and Isabel. That was not so odd as the convention appeared to be not to identify the offspring of baronets' siblings. There was at least one child, though, and that was Hester's mother. And Isabel must have been the 'woman of means' Hester mentioned her grandfather had married and who had shared the Camden house with him.

So, Hester – and Rachel, come to that – were descendants of the Assendenes. Neither had mentioned the fact. Rachel had even confirmed, without further comment, that Assendene Court was where the fire had taken place. Perhaps she did not know about the link with house and family; the maze symbol had sparked not a flicker of recognition. Or maybe he was wrong to assume that Lionel had married only once and there was no Assendene connection at all. And then he remembered Hester's reaction to the postcard of the maze and her taut suggestion that they 'had better have another chat'.

He went back to the journal, to the pages towards the end before the entries stopped. He was struck even more forcibly by the matter-of-factness of Lionel's account of the fire and its aftermath and the absence of umbrage or complaint. Surely the experience had some effect on him, an ordeal by fire that nearly killed him, even if he had come to no physical harm. Perhaps he found some other outlet. Certainly, the maze drawings became looser, wilder, almost frenzied, the hedges alight, the statue in the middle surrounded by a circle of flame, like Lionel himself. Pan looking as malevolent as he had the day Hugh too had felt trapped, confined by a circle of yew.

He turned over to the first blank page. At least, it looked blank. There was nothing drawn or written directly on it. But there was something all the same. He twisted his desk lamp to alter the beam. He could make out slight dents or impressions in the paper, a trace of markings on a previous page that had been removed. He took a pencil from the pot on the desk and rubbed the side of the lead gently over the marks. Gradually, the symbol of a maze was revealed and, beneath it, three words in aggressive block capitals:

THE AMBER MAZE.

That name again, the letters partly scored through. Hugh pulled open the bottom drawer of the filing cabinet, removed a sheet of paper and unfolded it at his desk. The watercolour of the maze they had found in Lionel's box. Even as a photocopy, it looked fresh and bright as it glowed in the concentrated beam of the lamp. The sheet simply had 'The Maze' at the bottom; there was no reference to amber but perhaps the intense orange-yellow of the painting made that unnecessary. Had Lionel painted it himself? It was done with great care and precision, unlike the freer sketches in the journal, and the words in sharp black copperplate gave nothing away about the hand that had been at work.

Kate was due to ring when she and the girls were on the train. There was still time. He put the sheet back in the drawer with the journal and turned to the computer. He had not yet pursued Anthony's suggestion of looking at Gavels' website for examples of Lionel's work in later life.

Four lots came up, none recent. All sold but at prices well below estimates that themselves seemed low to Hugh. He clicked on each of the images in turn, enlarging them as much as he could. Three of the pictures were untitled abstracts, bold rectangles, squares and triangles of colour, each shape crisply delineated. They were initialled 'LP' and dated variously in the late 1950s and early 1960s. They reminded him, a bit, of paintings by Mondrian and Ben Nicholson that he had seen some years ago at the Courtauld.

The fourth picture was quite different in style, a watercolour in fiery oranges and reds, again untitled but possibly a sunset, according to the catalogue. It was neither signed nor initialled and had no date. The picture was attributed to Lionel Pybus on the basis of the label on the back.

There was nothing on the website about the artist, except for his dates: 'Lionel Pybus (1890 – 1969)'. That made him about twelve when he stayed at Assendene, started the journal. Was there anything else about him online?

Very little, it seemed. There were no other auction records but there was a brief biography on the website of a gallery in Suffolk that had no works currently for sale but showed one sold work: another abstract (price unspecified) similar in feel to the ones he had seen before. The biography confirmed Lionel's dates and continued:

Born in Tooting, south London. Painter in oils, gouache and watercolour, notably of abstracts. Early career in journalism. Studied briefly at Summerstown School of Art but largely self-taught. Tutor at Chelsea School of Art before and after the Second World War and subsequently at Wimbledon. Exhibited at several London galleries, including Zwemmer, Beaux Arts, Walker's and Azimuth, and at the Royal Academy Summer Exhibition. Retrospective exhibition at the Black Box Gallery, his only recorded one-man show. Lived in London.

Not a lot about a life. There had to be more, surely. He started with the galleries mentioned but they had closed long ago. His train of thought was broken by the crash of the front door, followed by calls and whooping. They were back.

"We bumped into Sue at Victoria," said Kate. "She gave us a lift from the station so we didn't need to ring you. She's staying for supper."

He admired two identical pairs of pink ballet shoes, which the girls insisted on wearing for the rest of the day. Rosie's attempted entrechat proved a little ambitious while Eleanor made herself giddy by pirouetting up and down the hall. Hugh retreated to the kitchen.

After supper, Sue picked up one of the coasters scattered on the coffee table and turned it slowly in her hands.

"Anthony said he had a book with this maze mark

on the cover. When I was here last time. Did you go and see it?"

"I did; and brought it back for closer scrutiny. He wouldn't take any money for it. That makes it a gift; the Roberts Rule only applies to purchases."

Kate did not rise to the bait.

"What is it? asked Sue. "A Shakespeare First Folio?"

"Sadly not. It's a journal, I suppose. Written by a schoolboy over a century ago. Illustrated by him too. It seems he stayed at Assendene Court; that's where the coasters came from."

"May I see it?"

Sue took the burgundy volume and started to look through it while Kate went to make the coffee. She dwelt on some passages, skipped others, and ran her eye over the sketches.

"That was one troubled child," she said at last. "Quite sophisticated in some ways, painfully naïve in others. I wouldn't give much for his chances in the school playground. He was a talented artist too, if you ignore the weird ones."

She removed, without comment, the Ceylon hotel menu that Hugh had slipped in at the end and turned the open journal towards the light. She frowned and started to pick at the inside. Or so it appeared. Where the rear endpaper met the rear board was a narrow slit that he had not noticed and was not likely to be noticed unless the board was held down flat to expose it. A sheet of paper, identical to all the others, was pasted on to the three outer edges of the board but only part of the inner edge, the unpasted portion forming the slit. He had seen something similar in old travel guides as a way of containing a map or plan. But they were designed to be obvious and the contents easily removed.

Sue inserted the tips of forefinger and thumb carefully into the slit, using her nails as pincers to draw out what was inside. It was a note, unsigned, undated.

> *Welcome to The Amber Maze. Instructions will follow in due time, accompanied by a seal and sealing wax for use when required.*

Twelve

Hugh was looking out of the window of his fourth-floor office, the roofs below glazed with recent rain. He was lucky to have an office at all. The Commission's new Chief Executive was threatening to extend open plan to the few senior staff who had managed to escape its reach. A copy of her latest memo on the subject lay on his desk. He was thinking about reading it before his next meeting, the one about developing a strategic approach to the restoration of tapestries and other wall-hangings, when his temporary secretary, Caroline, put her head round the door and said there was a woman on the phone for him.

"Does she have a name?"

Caroline consulted her pad.

"Emily Coote?"

"I don't think I know her."

"That's what she said; that you don't know her?"

"Did she say what she wants?"

Caroline consulted her pad again.

"She says she's ringing from Assendene Court?"

"I'll take it."

Emily Coote, it turned out, was the archivist at Assendene. She apologised for not having been in touch earlier. She had returned from extended leave to find a message from 'poor old Simon' asking what information they had about Lionel Pybus. The acting house manager knew nothing about it. It was Pamela Quince, the manager of the shop, who suggested that the request might be for him, Hugh.

"I gather she met you that day."

He confirmed that Simon Marmion had been asking on his behalf and outlined what he thought he knew about Lionel's connection with Assendene.

"That's about right but I think we can put some flesh on the bones. Leave it with me."

Hugh still felt obscurely guilty about Simon, as if the manager's death after showing him round was in some way his fault. And after they found him in the library, it was Pamela Quince who took charge, called the ambulance, rung Simon's wife, though she said she was grateful for his moral support until it was time to close the house for the night. The funeral was a small family affair.

He had never mentioned that he got lost in the maze, the panic as the walls closed in, and not simply because he should not have been there in the first place. Not even to Kate when he woke with a cry in the early hours. Just a nightmare, he said, as they curled up together and she rocked him gently back to sleep. In the last one, the hedges were in flames.

She had, of course, immediately made a connection between the reference to 'The Amber Maze' in the note Sue found and the plan he brought back from The Old Rectory.

"That's what Rosie said, wasn't it? Like grandma's amber brooch. By the way, I met Rachel Broadbent the other day outside the school. Her mother has been asking when you're going round for another chat. She didn't say what about."

He had not forgotten. The postcard of the Assendene maze he gave to Hester Badingham signalled that he knew more about Lionel Pybus than he had gleaned from her. How much should he say? Should he admit to having the journal and the hidden note, give them to her, share the results of his research? Should he wait to see what information Emily Coote dug up? But there was no knowing when she might get back to him and he could not leave Hester's request hanging for too long.

The simplest thing, he decided, was to see what she wanted to say and take it from there. If he could use scraps of information to steer the conversation, so much the better. The main thing was to keep it focussed on what he really wanted to know: what *was* 'The Amber Maze'? The note hidden in Lionel's journal suggested that it was more than the maze itself.

She was sitting in the garden of The Old Rectory, a

small figure on a large bench out of sight of the house. Despite the warmth of the day, one of those dry, sunny days of mid-autumn, she was well wrapped in quiet country wear, altogether more subdued than the last time he had seen her. The shimmering after-image of those Uzbek pantaloons had taken a while to clear.

She was staring at a scattering of leaves on the grass in front of her and did not seem to hear him as he approached. And then, before he spoke, she looked up, a broad smile stealing across her pale face.

"I was thinking about January Cottage," she said. "The crab apple outside the kitchen window, the blackberries in the hedge at the end. Berries on the elders too, the pigeons perched for hours gorging themselves on fruit. Crab apple jelly, blackberry jam. We tried our hand at elderberry wine one year; all those plastic buckets and demi-johns. It wasn't a great success."

"You must miss the place."

"Yes, but I couldn't face another winter there by myself. I thought I'd better sell in summer while it looked its best and leave before my trip to the 'Stans. It was all rather a rush. As you see, I'm still here. For the time being."

"Not many crab apples or blackberries at The Old Rectory."

"The garden's much too tidy; you know where you are with it straightaway. There's no sense of mystery, no scope for discovery. They need an area to get lost in."

"Like a maze."

She patted the seat next to her and reached for the bag at her feet.

"Rachel said she'd given you the name of Assendene."

"The mansion, not the family. It was mentioned in some press cuttings about a fire at a country house. They were in the box. I just saw headlines and a few blurry pictures at the time. It was only later that I began to wonder where the place was and why Lionel had the cuttings. And kept them for the rest of his life."

"You've been there, I take it." She nodded towards the postcard she was holding, the one of the maze he gave her before.

"I had the opportunity when I was in Oxfordshire on other business. I learned a bit about the maze and the Assendenes themselves but it was not until I looked at the guide that I grasped that Lionel had married Isabel Assendene." He paused, then said gently, "Which must make you an Assendene too, at one or two removes."

"Yes."

"Rachel didn't seem to recognise the name, though she knew Lionel was her great-grandfather."

"We've never delved much into the family history. I must have explained about Lionel because she saw some of his paintings at the cottage."

"I knew from the date on the cuttings that the fire was in 1902. I assumed at first it was the house itself that caught alight but it turned out to be the maze – the original maze, that is. It was destroyed. There was a plan of a maze in the box and a seal too. The seal looks the same as the maze symbol used at Assendene. All of which made me think that Lionel must have known the place long before he married Isabel." He kept to himself the journal evidence of Lionel's schoolboy visit – and the note Sue had found. "Perhaps I'm trying to connect things that aren't related at all."

She did not respond and to fill the silence he said, "Of course, the answers may lie in the box." He recalled the piles of papers and photographs he had not had the chance to go through before. It was arguably none of his business but it was Hester who had asked *him* back and, according to Rachel, she had spent hours in her room looking at the contents of the box.

"Lionel died half a century ago," she said distantly. "He was a troubled man. He kept it well hidden until the last years of his life. Do you find it's getting chilly?"

To Hugh, the day seemed warmer than ever but he was content to adjourn to the summer house that overlooked the pond nearby. A weeping willow stood on the other side, its lower branches hovering above the surface of the water. Biscuits and a thermos of tea were already laid on, with milk in a small fridge disguised as a cabinet. He glanced at his watch; perhaps he had been wise to tell Kate he could be gone for a while.

Thirteen

I never knew how my grandparents met," said Hester. "At least, not while they were both alive. My mother said nothing about it, about the Assendene connection. She was their only daughter but she didn't seem close to either Lionel or Isabel. She hardly ever went to the Camden house, not even after Isabel died and he was living there by himself. I suppose I should have probed more, asked my mother what she knew. We always leave it till it's too late, don't we?"

She sighed and took a sip or two of tea. She stared through the open doorway of the summer house, saying nothing, as if she had forgotten that Hugh was there. Outside, strands of willow fluttered in a gentle breeze.

"It was one of the days I was in Camden Town. We'd been to the park and had stopped to look at the books on the junk stall at the corner of Inverness Street and Arlington Road. As we were coming away, I noticed a few people sniggering at a silver-haired man striding along Arlington Road swinging a tightly furled umbrella. He was tall and thin with a neatly trimmed moustache. And impeccably dressed: three-piece suit, carnation in his buttonhole, shiny black shoes, the lot. He looked very distinguished, a marked contrast to the flares and Afghan coats that seemed to be everywhere. When I pointed him out to Lionel, he went a deathly white and shot behind the nearest market stall. I'd never seen him move so fast. We went back to the house by a roundabout route, Lionel sending me ahead at every corner to check whether the man was there. All he would say was that the man reminded him of someone he had once known.

"Over the next few weeks, Lionel rarely ventured out during the day. I saw the man several times from a distance – he was unmistakable – but he never seemed to be doing much. Just standing and staring: by Henlys garage at the top of Parkway, outside Palmer's pet shop further down, on the bridge over the canal near Dingwall's timber yard, looking up at that statue of Cobden near Mornington Crescent. And then, quite unexpectedly, an encounter at close quarters. He was coming out of The Spread Eagle, only a couple of hundred yards from the house. He looked the same but there was something about him, a sort of quiet desperation, as if he had let his guard drop for a moment. And his carnation was wilting. The next thing I knew he was marching off towards the high street.

"I went into the pub to see if they could tell me anything about him. Turned out he always went there for a gin and tonic after he'd collected his pension from the post office. They regarded him as a local character, called him 'His Lordship'. Down on his luck, apparently, despite appearances. He had a cubicle at Rowton House, a big hostel for the homeless in Arlington Road, but had to be out during the day. They said the clothes he was wearing were the only ones he had."

The thought seemed to upset her, even at a distance of fifty years. She paused to finish her tea and accepted Hugh's offer to pour some more. He could think of nothing of substance to say and she did not seem to expect it.

"When I got to the house, I found that Lionel had closed all the shutters at the front. So that people couldn't see in, he said. Obvious nonsense after all the years he'd lived there with the shutters wide open; he could only have meant one person. I told him I'd seen the man leaving the pub and what they had said about him. '*His Lordship*? His name's Cecil Collingwood and he was standing on my steps not two hours ago. I hid upstairs until he'd gone.'

"He asked me to help him down with the box, the one I have now. Bit by bit, the story began to emerge. I'd forgotten many of the details but looking through those papers again brought everything back."

She confirmed that Lionel met Freddy Assendene at Broomwood Lodge, their prep school in Kent. He was invited to spend half-term at Assendene Court where he first saw Isabel, Freddy's younger sister. An incident cut the visit short and Lionel went home; he did not see Freddy or Isabel for several years.

"They didn't go back to school after half-term?"

"Lionel did but Freddy didn't return. His parents found him a private tutor; the boys went on to different schools when the time came. It was thought better that they should not meet."

"Because of the incident?"

"Yes."

"Would this relate to the fire in the maze? The timing seems about right."

"Freddy set light to the maze while Lionel was in it. Whatever Freddy's intention, Lionel was lucky to escape with his life. He never forgot it. The incident haunted him for the rest of his days. He had nightmares for years afterwards, used to wake up screaming that he was being consumed by fire. Eventually, Isabel was there to comfort him. She understood."

"But they weren't married until 1920, according to the guide. That's nearly twenty years after the fire."

"A few others along the way were briefed as circumstances required – school matrons, house masters and the like – but it was hardly the same."

"What about his parents?"

"He rarely saw them. His father was a tea planter in Sri Lanka – Ceylon as it was then – and his mother was out there with him. Lionel lived with a maiden aunt in Tooting; she tolerated him but not much more. It was a lonely childhood."

He thought of the menu from the hotel in Colombo slipped into the journal Anthony had given him. But he was not ready to reveal that he had it. Better, he felt, to hear what she had to say and offer prompts or steers if needed.

"Didn't his painting provide an outlet?"

"The painting came later but there are drawings from that time, dozens of them, some loose, some filling sketch books. And all depicting the maze before, during and after the fire. They're quite disturbing, particularly the ones showing a small figure trapped by flame. You can feel the sense of helplessness and panic."

"There was a plan of a maze in the box, the same shape as the one at Assendene. But that was neatly done in orange watercolour. If orange it is; one of my daughters said it was more like amber."

"That has nothing to do with it," she snapped.

She apologised and then, as if to lighten the mood, reached into the bag at her feet and pulled out a photograph.

"This may amuse you."

It was a dog-eared polaroid, faded, almost leached of colour, showing a girl with long hair and a short skirt swinging from a lamp post.

"This is me in the late 1960s on my way to a Beach Boys concert. It was at the old Astoria in Finsbury Park," she said distantly. "The place became better known as the Rainbow."

He struggled to find any resemblance. Perhaps the eyes, the nose. And, for a split second, the image of Isabel as she appeared in the drawings in the journal.

"You haven't changed a bit."

★

"Things began to happen in 1910," she said. "Lionel bumped into Isabel and her mother in the Army and Navy in Victoria Street. They had tea together and he learned that Freddy was at Oxford, having scraped in to read Theology, of all subjects. Freddy's declared ambition was to get a Fourth. It had a certain cachet in his set, apparently, requiring fine judgement or a lot of luck. A First or Second was considered much too serious, a Third merely dull. Isabel was languishing at Assendene between trips to France and Italy. When they finally asked Lionel what *he* was doing he felt obliged to reveal that he was at Oxford himself, reading English; he was only down in London for the day.

"No more was said at the time."

★

It is eight years since I last saw Isabel. I have often wondered what she would look like now and I am ashamed to admit that I did not recognise her at first. The long dark tresses that I remembered were piled beneath a broad-brimmed hat only a little less extravagant than her mother's confection of feathers and fruit. The brim of her hat cast a shadow over her pale skin when she lowered her head as if fleeting glimpses of her face were as much as I was allowed. But they were enough. She is radiant!

I felt as tongue-tied as the schoolboy I was at Assendene. Our conversation, with Lady A between us, was a little forced and platitudinous but both seemed keen that I should come to tea when Isabel is back from Rome, Florence, Venice and all the other places she mentioned. I cannot remember what they were. They did not ask after my drawing and it did not seem right to mention it.

The envelope appeared in my pigeon hole three days after my London visit. In the bottom righthand corner, the sender's name: *Hon. F.R.R. Assendene, M.H.* I knew Freddy was at Martlet Hall but was not sorry that our paths had somehow failed to cross. I was feeling apprehensive as I borrowed a knife from the buttery to slit open the envelope. Inside there was an invitation to a 'small dinner party' in Freddy's rooms. Nothing else. To be honest, I was reluctant to go but I reckoned that, since Freddy knew where I was, and had made the effort to get in touch, I could not put him off indefinitely. And a reconciliation with Freddy might make it easier to see Isabel when she is back. So, I borrowed a dinner jacket, dress shirt and bow tie and turned up at the appointed time.

We were six in all, including me. I didn't recognise the other guests, apart from Cecil Collingwood. I have not seen him since we left Broomwood Lodge. He seems taller and thinner than ever. He is not at Oxford and was vague when I asked him what he is doing now. 'Just something in the City' he said airily; that was as far as he would go. It was not clear why he was at the dinner party but then it was not clear why any of us was there.

The evening passed pleasantly enough. I plucked up

courage to join in the conversation after my second glass of claret. No one laughed when I said I liked to cycle out of Oxford and spend time with my sketch book. All the same, I felt I was under scrutiny in some way. Freddy and two of the others ended up in the pond in the front quad. Happily, there was no expectation that I would join them, or pressure to do so, and no one tried to throw me in.

Another envelope has arrived – without the sender's name. Instead, a seal in bright red wax, the mark resembling nothing so much as the maze I have tried to leave behind. I was shaking as I took the envelope back to my room to open. No invitation this time; just a note welcoming me to The Amber Maze.

★

"Did the note explain what that meant?" asked Hugh.

"Lionel said he might have assumed it was the name of a dining club, comprising or including the people he had met in Freddy's rooms. But he remembered the name from that awful day at Assendene, the day Freddy had said it was time for him to join his secret society. He didn't, of course, but it seems things were merely held in abeyance."

"But why should Lionel want to have anything to do with it? You said he never forgot being trapped in the maze and woke up screaming for years afterwards."

"I did but Freddy always had a hold over Lionel and he went about it quite cleverly, piquing his interest and reeling him in step by step, without any demands or apparent expectations. The note just said that instructions would follow, together with seal and sealing wax for use when required. There were no explanations and nothing about timing."

"And then?"

"A request to attend a meeting of 'the group' in Freddy's rooms."

★

It was late afternoon, approaching sunset, when I reached the bottom of staircase XII. I creaked up to the first floor; before I could knock, the door opened and Freddy led me in to the sitting room I had last seen arranged for the dinner party. The curtains were drawn and there was no light apart from the glow of the fire in the grate and what was given out by two large candles. One was on a round table in the middle of the room, the other on the mantelpiece illuminating a photograph of a statue I did not know.

As my eyes adjusted, faces emerged from the gloom. Men sitting in chairs, perched on window seats, a few standing. One chair remained empty. Freddy told me to take it while I was introduced to the assembled company. Freddy did not reciprocate at that stage by introducing them to me. Admittedly, I had met one or two of them at the dinner party but most were unknown to me. Cecil Collingwood was conspicuous by his absence but I suppose it is more difficult for him to get to Oxford.

There was absolute silence as Freddy began to speak. He no longer played the overgrown schoolboy or the amiable buffoon but came over as a figure of real authority, the leader of a secret society. Someone you would not cross with impunity. He had no title, like Great Vizier or Grand Master. He didn't need one. He just was and we all knew it. The transformation was extraordinary and not a little disquieting.

The society had no hierarchy, he said, with ranks or grades, though each member had his part to play. He announced that it was time for me to play mine. The man nearest the photograph of the statue was instructed to bring it to the table. Freddy said it was the statue of the goddess Angerona, with her mouth bandaged and a finger raised to her lips. 'The goddess of secrets and silence.'

And then I was required to swear an oath to Angerona that I would reveal nothing about the society, its membership or activities on pain of death.

★

"On pain of death? Freddy was joking, surely," said Hugh.

"He was perfectly serious."

"And Lionel went along with this?"

"He felt he had no choice but, like you, he thought it was just a piece of theatre. At the time. When he realised that the oath meant what it said, it was too late."

"And the other members had sworn this oath?"

"So it seems."

"No doubt thinking it was part of the game. But they only had to keep quiet."

"Perhaps they did not all grasp that simple point. Once Lionel had sworn, Freddy declared him to be a full member of The Amber Maze and presented him with the promised seal and sealing wax for use on society correspondence, together with an amber-coloured sash for wearing on ceremonial occasions."

"No other uniforms or regalia?"

"Freddy felt these should be kept to a minimum to avoid arousing unwanted attention. All letters using the seal were anonymous, just in case."

"What about the ceremonial occasions?"

"Presented as meetings of a dining club. They did not stint themselves when it came to food and drink and Freddy paid the bills."

"What was Lionel's role?"

"He was declared Keeper of the Book of Acquisitions. It was the one post in the society known to the other members; otherwise, who did what was kept deliberately vague. His job was to keep a brief note of the society's activities and to record, by way of drawings and sketches, a series of objects acquired on missions carried out on Freddy's orders. It was a position of considerable trust, giving an overview enjoyed by no one else but Freddy, and it caused some resentment."

"Lionel was recruited for his ability to draw?"

"Mainly."

"And the Book?"

"A leather-bound volume with the maze symbol on the cover, so Lionel said. Provided by Freddy."

"What happened to it?" It had not been in the box when he went through it with Rachel.

"Its whereabouts are unknown, if it survived. I've never seen it."

Fourteen

*T*hey resumed in Hester's small sitting room on the first floor. Rachel had flushed them out of the summer house and taken away the tea things. The bright day was fading fast and Hester was looking drawn. A circuit of the pond revived her and by the time they reached the house she was positively perky. She paused to lift a bottle and two glasses from the kitchen before heading for the stairs.

It was an odd little room, with doors off both sides as well as the one they had used to enter from the landing. Hugh wondered what its original function could have been; perhaps a dressing room or a nursery. There was little evidence of Hester's occupation. He doubted that the ranks of framed prints – Redouté roses to the left, Audubon birds to the right – had anything to do with her. Of the box and its contents there was no sign.

She waved him to a chair and took the one opposite, fumbling with a table lamp as she directed him to deal with the wine.

★

"I haven't grasped what this group or society was for or why anyone should want to join it," said Hugh. "Even if they did treat the oath as a joke."

"Freddy claimed he was establishing a network of like-minded people who would prove useful to each other in years to come. With some exceptions, they were recruited from a narrow social circle. Despite their privileged backgrounds, he had a way of making them feel special, set apart from their peers, chosen to be members of The Amber Maze and marked out for something more. I suppose they felt flattered. And I expect it helped that Freddy was paying the bills.

"He said that selection was merely a preliminary assessment, an indication of potential. This had to be tested in order to get a better feel for their individual skills and qualities and thus the contribution they might make to the wider effort 'in due course'."

"Were there no rules or a constitution? Something to give this society a bit of shape and focus."

"Nothing was written down, except what was recorded in the Book of Acquisitions."

"He wasn't striving for world domination or the downfall of Western civilisation, I take it?"

"Nothing like that. Lionel came to suspect that Freddy created the whole thing for his own amusement, as an antidote to a conventional, if well-heeled, upbringing and the prospect of many more years of the same. A fantasy, so to speak, to give him a sense of power and control over others, who were bound by an oath of secrecy not to reveal what he made them do. When he started the thing as a school boy, it involved nothing more serious than getting people to burn the bails before a cricket match or tie a ribbon on the tail of the headmaster's dachshund in return for something extra from the tuck shop. At Oxford, he decided to become more ambitious but nothing much happened before he hit on the idea of bringing Lionel into the fold. The Book was purely for Freddy's gratification: a record of what he had persuaded people to do by way of the tests he set them."

"Setting light to the maze was pretty serious."

"But that was Freddy himself, near-fatal as it was. The tasks he set others were rather different. Freddy took a particular delight in seeing them chronicled in the Book, to such an extent that the Book itself became the driver, or so it seemed to Lionel, as if Freddy was ordering things to be done just so that he could see them recorded there."

"As if the Book had an appetite of its own that needed feeding."

"Exactly, but for the Book read Freddy's megalomania. Of course, whatever it was fed was never enough."

Rachel appeared with nuts and olives. She said Kate had been asking about progress as Hugh was not answering his phone. He looked at Hester, who announced that he was staying for supper with her. He had neither the heart nor the energy to demur. Rachel departed to pass on the news while he prepared to spear an olive.

"What were these tests or tasks?" asked Hugh.

"Finding objects that Freddy specified and bringing them to him. Small things that could be procured and brought to his rooms in Martlet Hall without being too conspicuous."

"Such as?"

★

Freddy liked to start with something straightforward, like a jar of marmalade from Frank Cooper's shop in the High or a pair of pigskin gloves from Elliston's. He then upped the ante: a gold bracelet and a watch from the jewellers near Martlet Hall, rare books from Blackwell's, some ivories and jade from the Pitt-Rivers. Even a flag flying from a church tower on St George's Day. He summoned me every so often to log the objects in the Book, together with the date and place of acquisition and the initials of the acquirer – and to make drawings or sketches of them.

It was not too demanding but I felt uneasy all the same. Freddy was unmoved when I suggested that the tests amounted to theft. 'Not at all,' he said. 'We are no more than snappers-up of unconsidered trifles. Not even that. The acquisitions are only temporary. Think of them as loans, old man.' I had failed to grasp that the real test was that objects had to be returned by the people who acquired them, with Freddy himself making random checks that things were back in place.

★

"Easier to put some things back than others," said Hugh. "Wasn't anyone caught?"

"There were near misses, I believe, but security was a good deal lighter in those days and people more trusting of Varsity types."

"Was Freddy making things up as he went along or was there a grand plan?"

"The former presented as the latter was Lionel's view. Anyway, after a few months, Freddy began to get bored, though the members involved apparently found the risk-taking exhilarating and were keen to do more. In the first instance, he got Lionel to send an anonymous letter to the editor of *The Oxford Times* reporting the strange goings-on in the city, believed to be orchestrated by a criminal mastermind operating from within the university. This was designed to resolve the tension between Freddy's desire for some sort of recognition of the activities of The Amber Maze and maintaining its secrecy. In any event, it fell flat on its face. Nothing appeared in the newspaper. Perhaps because the letter was anonymous, perhaps because none of the shops or institutions involved had reported anything missing. I dare say the whole thing was considered a hoax.

"Freddy wanted to move on from glorified shoplifting. The appeal of acquiring inanimate objects lost its lustre; for him, at any rate. He set his sights on animate ones."

"Raiding pet shops? Hard to lift a puppy or a caged bird discreetly, let alone put it back."

"Freddy was inspired – if that's quite the right word – by the so-called outrages at Great Wyrley in Staffordshire some years earlier. Slashing of horses, cows, sheep. They achieved some notoriety, especially after Conan Doyle became involved in the case of George Edalji, convicted for injuring a pony."

"*Arthur & George*! I've read the book. But you're not saying that Freddy started to order the mutilation of animals. In the middle of Oxford."

"He demanded certain *parts*, shall we say, that would have required fairly horrific injuries of cattle, in particular. He claimed that this was readily achievable, given the cattle market there was then at Gloucester Green and the cattle grazing in Christ Church Meadow. Doing it in broad daylight was patently absurd, grotesque at any time, and the parts were hardly things like a jar of marmalade that could be put back later. Several members of the society refused to have anything to do with it. One or two others, it seems, delivered the goods by bribing a butcher's boy in the covered market to procure the necessary."

"Enterprising, if nothing else. Was Lionel expected to draw these…items?"

"He was and went along with it at first, with great reluctance. But Freddy wasn't satisfied with what was brought to him, started complaining of disloyalty and lack of resolve. He told those who wanted to resign that they could not do so, said they were members for life, and reminded them that they were bound to secrecy by the oaths they had sworn. Short-term qualms, he declared, could not be allowed to undermine the longer-term objectives of the society."

"Was anyone convinced? Sounds like it was Freddy's own authority that was being put to the test."

★

Cecil Collingwood, it seems, has no such scruples. He now has a car and drove, with two other members in tow, to an isolated field somewhere between Oxford and Assendene. Freddy knows the farm and told them where to go. They carried out his instructions, using implements Cecil brought from London, and arrived at Freddy's rooms with a canvas bag.

I was summoned 'to perform my duties as Keeper of the Book of Acquisitions' but when I saw what was involved – not to mention the smell – I refused, saying I was going to be sick. In the warm weather we have been having the contents, wrapped only in newspaper, had begun to go off. Even Freddy felt he had little choice but to get rid of the stuff as quickly as possible. He tipped it into the river in the early hours and climbed back into college.

I expected a tirade about 'disloyalty and lack of resolve' but nothing was said. I was summoned again a few days later. Freddy was in high good humour. The gruesome incident in the farmer's field was reported in two Oxfordshire newspapers and even had a paragraph in *The Times* drawing parallels with what had happened in Great Wyrley. He was particularly pleased by references to the apparent absence of motive and the bafflement of the police as to 'the perpetrators of this ghastly act of mutilation'.

★

"Recognition of a sort, I suppose," said Hugh.

"And a validation of Freddy's influence over others. In his own eyes, at least. He told Lionel to stick the cuttings in the Book, together with the initials of those involved."

"He knew whose initials they were?"

"And who was represented by all the other sets of initials recorded in the Book. There was a fair amount of duplication, of course."

"But this involved more than taking objects and putting them back. He had information that could have been of use to the police."

"He had no intention of doing anything with it. As he came to realise, though, not all the people concerned felt sure they could rely on his silence, despite the oath he had sworn."

The bottle that had surely been full when Hester swiped it from the kitchen now appeared to be empty. The nuts and olives had vanished too. Hugh began to feel woozy as the wine went to his head. Hester, on the other hand, sharper and more focussed than ever, seemed bedded in for the duration. He wondered at her powers of recall, even if she had spent hours going through the papers in Lionel's box. It was fifty years since those conversations in the Camden house; the

102

events Lionel had recounted took place another fifty or more years earlier. Perhaps the contents of the box confirmed what he had told her.

"Where did all this leave The Amber Maze?" asked Hugh.

"There was a restlessness in the group, a feeling that Freddy was going too far in his demands. He decided to put the tests on hold and focus on the social side for the time being. Finals were looming in any case and most of the members thought they should do some work."

"Even Freddy?"

"He opened several books, I believe, but not much more. He didn't want to prejudice his chances of getting a Fourth."

"While Lionel was up to his ears in *Beowulf* and *The Anglo-Saxon Chronicle*."

"He didn't spend all his time in the library."

An invitation to lunch at the Randolph with Freddy and his mother. It is the first time I have seen her since the chance meeting in the Army and Navy. Tea at Assendene has not materialised; Isabel, it seems, is recovering from her lengthy Italian trip by staying with her Aunt Violet at Menton. 'She speaks well of the climate and of the view over the bay from her balcony. So many palm trees!'

Lady Assendene was a little vague when I asked when Isabel would be back and steered the conversation to other matters. Freddy was on his best behaviour and very nearly treated me as if I were an equal. I was surprised when he addressed his mother by her Christian name: Olivia. She did not seem to mind. Does he call his father 'Ralph'?

Afterwards, Lady Assendene expressed an interest in seeing the majolica in the Ashmolean and asked if we would like to join her. Freddy said he'd give it a miss, if it was all the same to her, and made off towards the Broad. I rather think it was the answer she was expecting. That left me. My silence was taken as consent and we crossed the road. I was not sorry to delay my appointment with *The Battle of Maldon*.

Her interest in the pottery proved short-lived. She asked me about my own drawing and suggested that I do a sketch of her. A surprise present for her husband, she said. She had 'taken the precaution' of booking a room at the Clarendon Hotel in Cornmarket where she was 'less well known than at the Randolph'. When I said I had neither pencils nor sketch pad she replied that I would find everything I needed in the room. I do believe that Lady Assendene was as nervous as I was.

★

"Lionel actually did her portrait?" asked Hugh.

"Oh, yes. And others when she came to Oxford afterwards without troubling Freddy. But she took a somewhat broader view of the curriculum, as it were, and found Lionel a willing pupil. After a tentative start."

"At the Clarendon?"

"And the Mitre on one occasion, he said. Then she stopped coming."

"Any reason?"

"Weeks later Freddy had him over to a lunch party at Assendene to celebrate his achieving a Fourth in Theology – he said it was worth twice as much, as a matter of arithmetic, as Lionel's Second in English. It was that sweltering summer of 1911 when the whole of England was dried to a crisp. Lionel walked to the house from Assendene station and arrived late and dripping. After his second glass of Pimm's he saw Lady Assendene walk slowly on to the terrace and take her place in the shade of a large umbrella. He understood why she no longer came to Oxford. Giles was born early the following year. Sir Ralph was said to be delighted."

"Let me get this clear," said Hugh through a mouthful of lasagne. The elusive Guy had been deputed to carry the supper tray and set things up in Hester's sitting room. "Freddy must have been your great-uncle, through Isabel, though you never knew him. Giles, on the other hand…"

"We just called him 'Giles'. He was happy with that. He staggered on to the mid-1960s. He only lived a year after he was forced to sell Assendene. He was worn out by trying to keep the place going and crushed by his failure to do so. It had been in the family for hundreds of years. But none of the rest of us could have taken on the house and the estate."

Hugh made a mental note to look more closely at the photograph of Giles in the guidebook.

"What happened to the contents of the house?"

"Some smaller items came to the remaining members of the family. Most of the rest was sold as a job lot to the new owners, Clive and Dolly Paragon, who planned to restore the place to its former glory."

"The stuff's still there?"

"As far as I know. When the trust took over years later they proposed to keep things much as they were, apart from a few adjustments to create a route for the public to wander through the house."

Hugh put the empty plates on the tray – Hester had done little more than pick at the salad – and poured the coffee. Then he settled back and said,

"Lionel eventually married Isabel but she doesn't feature much in his Oxford period."

"She stayed abroad most of the time, improving herself. Not that anyone had any expectations of her, beyond making a suitable marriage when the time came. I'm not sure that Lionel *was* regarded as suitable at that stage – he was hardly county and had no obvious prospects – or whether he was in the frame at all. He was pretty backward in coming forward. On the other hand, it is possible that Isabel confided her own feelings to her mother and that Lady Assendene saw advantage in ensuring that Lionel was, shall we say, proficient in more than drawing."

"Training him for Isabel?"

"Such things happen, I believe, though I'm not suggesting her mother was entirely selfless. At any rate, he put his training to good use before he met up with Isabel again. Or so he told me when he thought it no longer mattered.

"Isabel was the brightest of the Assendenes, if you ask me, but the focus was on Freddy as the one due to inherit the title and take over the running of the estate. As an interim measure, as it was seen at the time, he had some ill-defined job in the City, thanks to his father's contacts. He stayed up in town during the week at the family's flat in one of those gloomy mansion blocks near Westminster Cathedral. Lionel saw him occasionally; he'd started work at the *Wandsworth Borough News* and was back with his Tooting aunt for a while before renting rooms of his own."

"Any sign of the parents?"

"They were in England when his father had long leave before Lionel went up to Oxford. That was it for another five years. Such was the life of a tea planter. They were due back in 1913 but there was some hitch and then the war came. It must have been a good ten years before Lionel saw them again. He said they were strangers."

Neither of them said anything for a while. Hester seemed to be flagging and somehow looked smaller. He wondered where all this was going, how much more she had to say. He used the silence by asking,

"Was The Amber Maze defunct by this time?"

"Every six months or so envelopes arrived, sealed with the maze symbol, summoning members to dinner in the private room of one London restaurant or another: sashes to be worn. They were mainly social occasions but served to remind people that they remained a network for mutual co-operation and support, if required. Freddy insisted that the events, and the initials of those attending, were recorded in the Book."

"By Lionel, as Keeper."

"Indeed. No acquisitions to record in those years, of course, but it amused Freddy to remind the assembled company over the port of a selection of 'past triumphs', as he put it. It was Lionel's job to read these out from the Book. The names or initials of the perpetrators remained unspoken but that did not prevent some of those present from looking embarrassed or uncomfortable. And none more so than Cecil Collingwood and a couple of others at the final dinner before the war."

"The incident on the farm."

"They anticipated meeting early the following year after the war was over. Perhaps Freddy realised this might be optimistic because, as people were dispersing, he drew Lionel aside and handed him another book – for safe keeping. 'Just in case, old man. Wouldn't want it to fall into the wrong hands.' This was the Book of Members. It contained not only a complete list of members of The Amber Maze and their contact details – Freddy had demanded that he be kept up to date with their movements – but also pen portraits of each person. These included an assessment of their strengths and weaknesses based on performance of the tasks he had set, together with any other observations he cared to make about them."

"Including Lionel himself?"

"There must have been something, I suppose, but his role was primarily administrative; he was not set tasks in the same way as the others."

"Even so."

"Freddy joined up at the earliest opportunity. As the elder son of a prominent Oxfordshire family, there were certain expectations, though he claimed he was relishing the fight."

"Why should the Book have been any safer with Lionel? Wasn't he expected to join up too?"

"I dare say Freddy was happier leaving it with someone he felt he could trust – and who had taken the oath – than locking it in a desk drawer or a deposit box. Lionel already looked after the Book of Acquisitions in his role as Keeper."

"So much for spreading the risk."

"As it happens, Lionel did not fight. He was called up by the War Office to be a member of the Intelligence Corps, then a very small team. The man recruiting him said he knew from mutual acquaintances that he was reliable, a man who understood the need to be discreet. Lionel never spoke of what he did or where he did it but he was able to go to Freddy's funeral in 1916. He died at Verdun."

★

The funeral was at St Mark's in the village. There was a good crowd, all things considered. I managed to drum up a few members of The Amber Maze; many were away fighting and several had been killed. The Book of Members has become increasingly irrelevant.

If anything good can be said to have come of Freddy's demise it is that I was reunited with the rest of the family, including Isabel. Especially Isabel. She has trained as a nurse and is helping at Assendene. The place has been turned into a hospital for wounded soldiers. There are beds in the larger rooms, panelling boarded over and chandeliers bagged up, men convalescing on the terrace, and so on.

The loss of Freddy has hit his mother hard. She puts on a brave face and busies herself with good works around the county. The aged nanny has come back to look after Giles. That day, though, the day of the funeral, she pressed me to stay for tea with her and Isabel in the family apartment upstairs after everyone else had left. Sir Ralph found he had other things to do.

Lady Assendene thanked me for being friends with Freddy, particularly in view of 'past difficulties', but did not mention the times she had seen me in Oxford. Not surprising while Isabel was in the room but it was the same when I visited in the remaining years of the war. She remained wistfully distant. And yet, as I was leaving the apartment that time for a turn round the lake with Isabel, I caught a glimpse, on the walls of Lady Assendene's private sitting room, of sketches I had done of her. They were framed identically.

★

"Did he see much of Giles in this period?"

"I won't say they were deliberately kept apart; they just never happened to meet. Always the wrong moment, it seems. No opportunity for awkward comparisons. After Giles' mother died, he was sent away to school."

"Spanish flu, did I read?"

"Just as things were beginning to return to some sort of normality after the war. It was only a couple of years after Freddy went. Sir Ralph was devastated and retreated even further into his shell. Isabel, by contrast, became more outgoing, not that things had been quite as restrained during the war years as she liked to pretend. The boat house was not used solely for the storage of boats."

"So much restraint – or the appearance of restraint."

"Discretion, perhaps, rather than self-control. Anyway, things blossomed a little more openly in the months after the funeral. Isabel was even introduced to Lionel's parents and they came to Assendene."

"The strangers."

"I think they felt as awkward as he did after so long apart. He was a stranger to them too. But things mellowed during their stay and they managed to tell him how much they liked Isabel. And they told Isabel that they were proud of Lionel. She passed that on but he never heard it from *them*. He didn't see them again; they died of fever shortly after they went back to Ceylon."

"They missed the wedding."

"But at least they had met Isabel. That meant a lot to him. And they saw St Mark's when they were visiting Assendene. The church where the wedding took place.

"Lionel's inheritance bought them a place of their own and enabled him to give up the journalism and enrol at art school. Not that Isabel was short of a bob or two herself. Oh, and the Tooting aunt sold up and moved to Bognor with a man in the motor trade. She died at the age of ninety-five after choking on some candyfloss at the Festival of Britain."

Fifteen

I was about to send out a search party," said Kate.

Hugh slumped in a chair, head pounding, feeling drained.

"Why is it that women of a certain age feel the need to tell you their life stories?"

"I have a trustworthy face and a sympathetic ear," he said. "And I don't judge. There's no remedy; it's just the way I am."

He ignored the snort of derision and continued,

"Anyway, it wasn't *her* life story but her grandfather's. Or part of it. We'd only reached 1920, the year he was married, when she ground to a halt. I'm not surprised; she'd been talking virtually non-stop for hours."

"She hasn't finished?"

"Apparently not. There's more she wants to say. It's another fifty years' worth if we're going all the way but I had the impression that what she was telling me was by way of background to something specific."

And yet he also had the feeling that, despite the length of her account, she had been holding back, had been evasive in response to some of his questions. There were plenty of gaps too, not that he relished a blow-by-blow account of Lionel's undergraduate career or his work at the *Wandsworth Borough News*. Probably she had been spared those details herself and they did not serve her purpose in any event. If only he knew what it was.

"So how were things left? Are you going back for another marathon session?"

"The ball's in Hester's court. Rachel insisted that she went to bed and said she'd be in touch. She apologised for her mother keeping me so long. She may have been a bit upset that she'd been excluded from the process. I mean, why would Hester talk about family history to a stranger but not to her own daughter?" He wondered, not for the first time, whether Hester featured in Rachel's case notes. Pity they were locked away in Kate's consulting room at the Centre.

"We don't know what she's said to Rachel. But you must tell me what she told *you* sometime. Just the gist. Did you mention that journal of Lionel's you got from Anthony?"

"It never seemed the right moment. And I didn't want to interrupt what she wanted to tell me. Perhaps next time."

The bed-side clock glowed five to three. He had been awake for over an hour as his brain whirred with thoughts about what Hester had said and not said. Kate slept quietly beside him. He eased out of bed, fumbled for dressing gown and slippers in the faint green light and made his way to the study. The click of the desk lamp, the creak of the chair seemed unnaturally loud in the still, cold air. Three distant bongs from the tower of All Saints chided him for being here at all.

He wondered that Hester did not make more of the loss of Assendene, even if its upkeep was beyond the family. How did Lionel feel about it? Or Isabel, for that matter? She had known the place all her life. And Hester herself must surely have been there before it was sold in the mid-1960s. There was nothing to suggest she had been to Assendene since it was open to the public, taken Rachel or anyone else.

When *was* the trust set up? He reached for the guide teetering on the back edge of the desk and found what he wanted. The trust had been established in 1989 with the benefit of a substantial endowment from the estate of Dolly Paragon in memory of her late husband Clive. The couple had no children and had used the place for entertaining, letting it occasionally for weddings and corporate events.

He flicked to the section on the house in the years after the Second World War and the futile attempts to stave off the inevitable. An all-too-familiar country house story but no less poignant for that. There were two photographs of Giles: one as a young man, proud of his inheritance and the family's lengthy association with the place, determined to make a go of things; the other showing him haggard and careworn shortly before the Paragon sale. Yet both were recognisably the same man, the eyes and nose not dissimilar to Hester's own. Or Lionel's, come to that.

And then there were those books: the Book of Acquisitions and the Book of Members. Hester said she had never seen the first and had made no claims one way or the other about the second. They had not been in the box when he went through it with Rachel but it seemed unlikely that Lionel would have turfed them out, especially given some of the things he did keep. Mind you, the journal had not been in the box either and had apparently been mislaid by Hester in the muddle of the move from January Cottage.

He slid open the bottom drawer of the filing cabinet and removed the journal. He guessed that the missing volumes looked much the same: bound in burgundy leather with the maze emblem on the front cover, tooled in gold. Did Hester really not know where they were?

Hugh was recovering in his office from the Chief Executive's meeting on the Commission's aims and objectives for the next three years. He finished his coffee and was about to check the email when Caroline put her head round the door.

"It's that woman again? The one who rang before?"

"Which woman?"

Caroline consulted her pad.

"Emily Coote? The archivist at Assendene Court?"

"Put her through."

"Lionel Pybus came here for half a century or more,"

said Emily. "Particularly, of course, after he married into the family. Isabel's father remained for the best part of twenty years after she moved out. When Sir Ralph died, her brother Giles inherited the house and the title. Lionel and Isabel brought their daughter, Sophia. Years later, her own daughter, Hester, came too."

"How do you know all this? I mean, wouldn't the family papers have been dispersed when the place was sold or, at any rate, passed to the Assendene descendants. I know the Paragons bought a lot of the contents but surely that didn't include all the documents relating to the previous occupiers."

"The library itself remained intact when the Paragons arrived − and when they left. The books are still here and have been properly catalogued. Mainly of interest for the bindings. Standard country house fare of the fur, feather and fin variety with the usual helping of *Punch* and *Country Life* and a smattering of volumes that look as though they might have been read. Much of the family archive was deposited with the county record office in Sir Ralph's time. The archive goes back hundreds of years. More recent papers and photographs went to Isabel in the first instance."

"They weren't kept by Giles? Wherever it was he went."

"He retreated to the family's flat in Westminster. He had the space but he didn't want the responsibility. He wasn't well by this time, though, in the event, Isabel didn't outlive him by long. Things were stored in the house she and Lionel had in Camden Town and when

Lionel himself went at the end of the '60s. Sophia was persuaded to take them on."

"Persuaded by?"

"Her daughter, Hester, who seems to have been closer to Lionel than was Sophia. At that stage, I gather, Hester never lived anywhere for long and could not have housed the boxes in a bedsit anyway."

"Why didn't they join the rest of the archive in the county record office?"

"The people and events covered still seemed too recent, I expect, and not for prying eyes. They stayed with Sophia for about twenty years. She died at much the same time as the trust was set up. It was Hester's idea to give the material to us – bringing it back home, so to speak."

"All of it?"

"It's hard to say. This was well before my time and I'm relying on what my predecessor, Henry Marland, has told me. He wrote the first version of the Assendene guide. I took the precaution of rootling him out in his retirement. He still remembers Hester. She spent hours going through the stuff with him. There were one or two curiosities."

Sixteen

---

*I*t was a cold grey morning. The surface of the lake was pitted by rain and ruffled by an insistent breeze. A small flotilla of pedalos, firmly tethered to the boardwalk, bobbed and strained under the watchful eyes of a gaggle of Canada geese. A solitary heron stood motionless at the water's edge.

Nursing a paper cup of coffee in gloved hands, Hugh took shelter under the overhang of the pavilion that housed the Lakeside Café. He was the first – and, so far, only – customer of the day, having dropped Eleanor and Rosie at their ballet class and come straight here. It had been Hester's idea to meet on what she called 'neutral territory', on the basis that Rachel had put her foot down about snaring him again at The Old Rectory and it would not be right to corner him in his own home.

Where was she? He took a turn round the perimeter of the building, dodging drips and soggy dogs, until he was back where he had started. And then, as he looked idly through the misted windows of the café, he made out, settling into the corner furthest from the door, a small figure wearing a John Lennon cap. It was Hester.

As he entered the café, she signalled with her cap and half-rose to greet him. While he organised more coffee and a plateful of pastries, she twisted to open the large bag she had planted on the floor beside her.

"Guy left me by the gate," she said. "I was going to walk but what with the weather…I'm hoping it will discourage people from coming to the park. And there's the bag." She nodded towards the carpet bag gaping by her chair. "I've been busy but I had to be selective in what I brought. I'll give him a ring when we've finished.

"Rachel did tell me to cut to the chase. And so I shall. In just a minute."

She leaned forward and looked furtive.

"The other day, I spent some time in Camden Town. Revisiting the scene of the crime, as it were. Sad to see what's gone, cheering to see what's much the same. But the shops. Does anyone need so many tee-shirts? Lionel's house looks exactly as it did, apart from the yellow front door and the olive trees in pots at the front. It's the rest of the houses in the street that have been tarted up beyond recognition. I rather miss the mattresses and the cars up on bricks. Seemed more real, somehow. Oh, and I went with Rachel to that self-storage place. It took me a while to find things; I'd quite forgotten what was there. Where did we end up last time?"

"Lionel and Isabel had just got married and moved to London. He gave up journalism and went to art school."

"But not for long; when my mother Sophia was

born he took up teaching. He was barely qualified but a few people in positions of influence thought well of his work and secured him the job at Chelsea."

She delved into her bag and brought out a picture, loosely shrouded in bubble wrap. Two sketches of a baby girl, mounted together. Simply done with great delicacy and tenderness. They reminded him of the twins at the same age. He muttered something about paintings by Constable and Gainsborough of their own daughters that said far more than words ever could.

Hester released a quiet smile and left it a bit before slotting the picture back into the bag. Then she became brisk and said,

"It happened in 1935. Lionel was in the house by himself. They were still at Tooting in those days. Sophia was away at school, Isabel was at the hospital. She had gone back to being a nurse, building on her experience at Assendene.

★

I spotted it lying on the mat when I came down to make some lunch. Ensconced in my studio with the gramophone playing, I heard nothing. No footfall on the step, no clack of the letter box. It could have been there a few minutes or a couple of hours.

The envelope had landed face down so the seal was the first thing I saw. A red seal with the maze mark. And when I turned it over, there were only three words on the front: 'Mr Keeper Pybus'. In neat black italics. No address. No stamp. No indication of who had sent it.

I took the envelope to the kitchen and slit it open with a knife. The note inside said little, but enough.

You are cordially invited to a reunion of members
of The Amber Maze.
It has been too long.

It gave a date and time and a place, the private room of a restaurant in Soho. *Black tie; sash to be worn.* There was no means of replying and presumably no expectation that I would do other than be there. I rang the restaurant to find out who had made the booking; the manager regretted that he was unable to divulge the information over the phone.

I wondered who knew where I lived. Or had the addresses of the others whom I assumed had been invited to the reunion. The Book of Members was still locked in my studio with the Book of Acquisitions. But I soon realised that the simple expedient of looking at the London telephone directory would yield my details and no doubt those of other members too, though many had died in the war. I have lost touch with the survivors. Without Freddy to provide the impetus, nothing has happened and the network has effectively ceased to exist. Or so I thought.

It was a damp evening in November. I found the place easily enough: Le Brugnon in Greek Street. I was directed to a narrow staircase at the back of the restaurant. The room was on the first floor overlooking the street. On the tube, I tried to guess who would be there, having refreshed my memory before I set out by looking through the Book of Members. I started by eliminating the people I knew to have perished and a few others I had heard or read had moved abroad. That still left a fair number.

So when I knocked and went in I was surprised that the room was a small one. The table in the middle was set for only four. Three other men were already there. I was greeted effusively by that dapper giraffe, Cecil Collingwood! His head only just avoided contact with the ceiling. He took my coat and gave me a glass of champagne before allowing me to renew acquaintance with the two others present.

I am not the most clubbable of men at the best of times and I confess that I did have misgivings about attending the gathering, particularly given the way I was invited. But I was curious to find out what had become of people I had last seen before the war. In my mind's eye they were still in their early twenties, not well into middle age.

Charles Brandon I recognised immediately. The man had hardly changed at all. Not a hint of paunch or greying hair. However, I struggled with the third member of the trio: wheezy, red-faced, with the girth of an oak. Cecil intervened and reminded me that this was Quentin Rose, 'the distinguished Parliamentarian'. Conversation before and during dinner – sashes slipped on before we sat down – was inconsequential, a mixture of reminiscence and canter over what we had done in the quarter century since we had come down. Those with more active wars than mine held centre stage but they seemed genuinely impressed that I had married the sister of Freddy, whom we toasted as founder of The Amber Maze. When I said I had been expecting rather more of the old gang, Cecil claimed he had tried but failed to establish their whereabouts. I was less than convinced – and rightly so, as it turned out. Perhaps I should have realised sooner that invitations would not have been hand-delivered to members all over London and beyond.

When the brandy appeared, Quentin leaned forward, as best he could, and said, 'Some rather disturbing information has come to light.' He had received an anonymous letter suggesting that he had been involved in the mutilation of cattle on an Oxfordshire farm before the war. The letter further suggested that, were this to become public knowledge, it could prove unhelpful to his role as a Member of Parliament and especially to his position at the Ministry of Agriculture and Fisheries. It would be a pity to blight such a promising career. On the other hand, payment of the specified sum by the specified means would overcome these difficulties.

Quentin noted that, apart from himself, only four people knew he had performed the task. One was Freddy; the other three were in this room. Two of those – Charles and Cecil – were also involved in carrying it out and, he said, could be presumed to have maintained their silence, as indeed their oaths as members of The Amber Maze required. 'That leaves you, Lionel Pybus,

Keeper of the Book of Acquisitions with a finger in every pie baked on Freddy's behalf. Have you forgotten the oath and the punishment for breaking it?'

I said I had not even recognised Quentin. This was apparently regarded as simulation, on the basis that no one could possibly fail to remember a man whose photograph was frequently in the papers. I then reminded them that the incident had been recounted to other members at the last of Freddy's dinners in the Westminster flat. The trouble with that line was that the perpetrators had not been identified, as Quentin was not slow to point out.

So I emphasised that I had no possible motive and did not need the money, being married to a wealthy member of the landed gentry. A slight exaggeration but they were not to know. This appeared to give Quentin pause for thought. He said he would consider the matter further and conversation turned, rather awkwardly, to other matters while he and Cecil lit up cigars.

I wanted to leave but feared that a rapid departure would be seen as an admission of guilt. A quick get-away, as it were, though they knew where I lived, of course. After we left the restaurant, Cecil asked me which way I was going. When I said I was headed down the Charing Cross Road to Leicester Square station Cecil and Quentin said that they were too. Charles Brandon, who had looked uncomfortable throughout the interrogation and played no part in it, went his own way towards Soho Square.

At the station, I bought a ticket to Trinity Road

but I was destined never to use it. I took the escalator and then the stairs, still accompanied by the other two. They had tickets for Hampstead. At the bottom, we parted on apparently friendly terms as our trains were going in opposite directions: mine to Morden, theirs to Edgware. While I was waiting, I spent time flicking through a copy of *The Star* I found lying on one of the seats. When I heard my train approaching, I moved forward. I felt a hand grip my arm and drag me towards the edge of the platform. It was Cecil, who shouted to Quentin to grab my other arm as I struggled to shake him off. Quentin can't have been the most agile of men at the best of times and that evening had not stinted on the brandy or anything else in the liquid department. Perhaps he had been relying on Cecil to do the job and had not thought he would need to make a move himself. At any rate, he was slow and unsteady. As Cecil and I stumbled backwards, away from the platform edge, Quentin tripped over one or both of us, lost his footing and fell into the path of the oncoming train. He didn't even scream, having delegated that task, it seemed, to a woman further down the platform.

The train braked and screeched and bumped over the body. I shall not forget that sound; it haunts me still. Cecil got up, ran through to the other side and leapt on to a northbound train just as the doors were closing. I shouted to no one in particular that I would to go and get help, though I had no intention of doing so. I went back up and out into the night. My sole aim was to get away from the area as quickly as possible but I thought it best to walk over to Covent Garden before catching a taxi. I split the journey at Victoria and caught another one home to Tooting. It was some years before I used Leicester Square station again.

★

"He must have been in shock," said Hugh.

"You'd have thought so, and who better to go home to than a trained nurse. But he never told Isabel what had happened at the dinner or afterwards. Or so he said. He only told me when Cecil Collingwood turned up in Camden Town thirty years later."

"Did no one at the station give a description of Lionel – or Cecil? Cecil, at least, sounds rather distinctive."

"Apparently not. It all happened so quickly and the place was pretty deserted in the gap between the post-theatre crowds and the dash for last trains. Even the ticket collector had left his place at the top."

"What about the restaurant? They surely recognised Quentin Rose if his photograph was always in the papers."

"The manager came forward but neither he nor the waiter assigned to the upstairs room could give a coherent account of Quentin's fellow diners, other than that there were three of them and one was unusually tall."

"But Cecil booked the room."

"Under another name, it turned out, and paid in cash. It was all reported in the papers at the time."

"Charles Brandon could have come forward."

"He didn't. I dare say he saw nothing to gain by it. Perhaps he guessed, given what was said at the dinner, that Lionel was the intended victim."

"And the verdict?"

"In all the circumstances, it was convenient to record that death was accidental. There was no reason to suppose suicide and no proof of unlawful killing or apparent motive for it, even if the pair the woman on the platform thought she had seen had disappeared sharpish. It was evident from the post mortem that Quentin had had an awful lot to drink. A by-election took place shortly afterwards."

The rain was even heavier now, swelling from gutters and downpipes, drumming insistently on the café roof and the metal tables outside. The lake was barely visible through the curtain of grey that muted even the yellow pedalos thrashing on the surface of the water. Hugh and Hester had the place to themselves until a couple burst through the door, bringing cold air and wet leaves, and dripped to the corner furthest from them.

"Lionel carried on as if nothing had happened?"

"To all outward appearance, I imagine. But he was shaken by the unexpected turn of events and the realisation that the reunion dinner was arranged solely to ensnare him."

"That's putting it mildly."

"It was nothing about punishment for breaking the oath and everything about safeguarding Quentin's career and reputation."

"Except that Lionel played no part in the blackmail."

"He was worried that Cecil would turn up and try again. Or threaten Isabel and Sophia."

"Why would Cecil do that once Quentin was dead?"

"Revenge. Or unfinished business."

"I can't see why Cecil would take the risk. What was in it for him? Quentin's death wasn't Lionel's fault anyway. *They* bungled the attempt to dispose of *him*. You could argue that Cecil had more to fear from Lionel."

"Another reason for Lionel to be wary: the chance, however remote, of Cecil getting his retaliation in first. He toyed with the idea of getting in touch with Charles Brandon to see if he knew how the land lay but thought it better not to stir things up. As it happened, Charles appeared out of the blue a couple of years later. It was at the private view of an exhibition Lionel had with a few other artists at a small gallery in Fitzrovia. The Azimuth Gallery. It was in one of those streets off the Tottenham Court Road."

"Presumably not a coincidence, Charles turning up, if Lionel was on the billing."

"And with the benefit of safety in numbers from both their points of view. He took Lionel to one side and, after a few words about events on the evening they had last met, said he'd heard that Cecil was now in South Africa. It seemed that funds from the City bank at which he worked had gone with him. Charles said he strongly suspected Cecil of blackmailing Quentin himself, sending the anonymous letter and encouraging

Quentin to think that it could only have been sent by Lionel."

"Did he buy a painting?"

"He did – and a number of others over the years. Perhaps he felt guilty about his passive stance at the dinner and letting Lionel go off with the others afterwards. But he also became a friend, the only one Lionel had from the old days."

Hester dipped into the bag beside her and pulled out two more pictures. She raised them slowly to eye level, letting sheets of tissue paper rustle to the floor.

"Early Pybus on the right," she said. "Mid-period Pybus on the left."

Hugh took the first, an abstract done in watercolour, signed and dated 'LP 1921'. It comprised a series of concentric circles, possibly inspired by the maze symbol, divided into quadrants, each ring of each segment a separate but complementary colour. It was complex and busy but not frantic like the youthful sketches he had seen in the journal. The energy was restrained, the rhythm and movement controlled. The longer he looked at it the more he admired the skill with which it was composed and executed. It was hard to believe it was painted the same year as the drawings of Hester's mother as a baby he had seen earlier.

He exchanged it for the second picture she was resting on the table. Another abstract, again comprising geometric shapes but simpler, with circles taking second place to squares, rectangles, triangles. There were fewer colours and the painting had a more solid, more definite feel. Gouache rather than watercolour, by the look of it. In the bottom right-hand corner: 'LP 1937' and, on the back, a label: 'Azimuth Gallery, Windmill Street, London W'. Unsold?

"I don't understand why Lionel isn't better known," said Hugh. "Or known at all."

"He was a competent artist but he didn't break new ground. That was his own view. You can see the influence of others in his work. He was a discreet follower of continental artists of the day, appreciated by his peers and a few enthusiasts. Apart from the odd exhibition, he painted for his own satisfaction and didn't try to sell what he produced or seek publicity. He was indifferent to fame and fame was indifferent to him. He did do some illustrations for worthy but short-lived magazines in the late 1930s and, again, after the war but these too have been forgotten. Otherwise, he was content to help his students and take pleasure in their achievements."

"A complete waste," said Hugh, with more vehemence than he intended. "Didn't Isabel find it frustrating?"

"Intensely. She even visited galleries herself with examples of his paintings and, later, enlisted Charles' help to try to bring Lionel's work to a wider audience. Over the years, there was a lot of interest, at least initially. But he wouldn't play ball and enthusiasm waned. He was pleased to have a picture accepted for the Summer Exhibition but, typically, his only one-man show was after he died. That was at the Black Box in

1970, thanks to Charles. The gallery owner took armfuls from the studio in the Camden house, had them framed and, when those sold, came back for more. Several of the pictures were hung upside down but that didn't inhibit sales at all."

Hester turned and took one last picture from her bag.

"Behold a late Pybus," she said, with a flourish.

Initialled and dated 1960, it was similar to the paintings he had seen on Gavels' website, the minimalist ones that had reminded him of Mondrian and Ben Nicholson. They marked a further, and final, stage in the development of Lionel's abstract work.

Hugh looked at the picture for some minutes while Hester wrapped the others and put them back in her bag. Then he said,

"There has to be more to it."

"To what?

"Lionel's reluctance to put his head above the parapet. Surely any artist would relish wider recognition of his work. I don't mean fame and fortune, necessarily, but at least a proper appreciation of his talent, the knowledge that other people were enjoying what he did."

"He hated what he called 'pomp and circumstance'. It was drummed in to him early on by the Tooting aunt that he should not draw attention to himself and it suited him to adopt that stance in his school career. He kept his head down. He wasn't unpopular or without friends but he avoided being singled out. It was a question of survival in those establishments and then it became a habit."

"I don't suppose the maze incident helped."

"Two near-death experiences, one or both a deliberate attempt on his life. That one in 1902 and the botched effort on the platform more than thirty years later. A long time apart, with a world war between them, but both leaving a lasting impression. As you might imagine. He thought they were his own fault, that he had brought them on himself in some ill-defined way."

"How could they be his fault?"

"I don't know how he rationalised it, or if he did, but the incidents troubled him to the end of his life. There were sudden flashbacks, he said, that made him seethe with anger and drove him to acts of violence: hurling a plate against the wall, ripping pages from a book, even slashing a painting. I think it frightened him, although I never saw that side. To me, as to the outside world, he was the most placid and gentle of men."

"And to the rest of the family?"

"With Isabel, at least, he put it down to the fire in the maze. He had to tell her something. She knew about that already, of course, if not about the incident in 1935. She was a great comfort to him.

"And then she died and Cecil turned up again."

The rain had stopped. A shaft of sunlight glanced off one of the outside tables and dazzled through the café door, briefly illuminating a patch of floor before the clouds closed over. Hester, scrunched in her corner, seemed unsettled. She said she needed something stronger than coffee. Hugh procured two glasses of nameless house red and winced as he sipped. Hester was unfazed.

"Lionel knew that Cecil had come back from South Africa," she said, "but not that he was out of prison. Financial irregularities again; he always thought he could get away with it and he never did. That's what Charles told me later. When Cecil came to Rowton House, the hostel in Arlington Road, I don't think he had any idea that Lionel was living in Camden Town and had been since he retired from teaching in the 1950s."

"But didn't you say that he saw Cecil standing on his front steps?"

"My guess is that Cecil spotted Lionel in the area by chance and tailed him back to the house."

"No malicious intent?"

"I doubt it. It was more than thirty years since the dinner in Soho and what followed it. And what would he have done? He must have been in his mid-seventies at least. Lionel didn't see it like that, of course, and couldn't face the prospect of spending his days hiding in the house until Cecil moved on."

"What did he do?"

"He took to following Cecil himself, to see if he could establish a pattern in the man's movements. It became something of an obsession."

"Didn't Cecil know he was being followed?"

"If he did, he didn't let on. Whether it influenced what he did, where he went, I don't know. Perhaps it amused him to think he was wasting Lionel's time. At any rate, Lionel discovered that, every Thursday night,

Cecil went to the Mixer, the pub close to the hostel, where he was bought a few drinks in exchange for regaling the assembled company with stories of his exploits in South Africa and elsewhere. Apocryphal, no doubt, but entertaining. Afterwards, he made a circuit of the area before returning to the hostel. Always the same route, Lionel keeping up as best he could. He was fit for his age but found it hard to match Cecil's stride.

"And then one evening Cecil veered off course and headed towards the bridge over the canal. Lionel lost him, he said, near Dingwall's timber place. Perhaps he was hiding in the shadows, waiting for Lionel to go."

"Or to confront him, particularly if he knew he was being followed."

Hester shrugged. "Cecil found a way into the site at some point. I assume he spent his remaining time skulking or wandering the cobbled yards between the warehouses."

"Remaining time?"

"He was discovered in the morning. Face down in the canal, the papers reported, hard up against the bank. When he was pulled out and turned over there was a carnation still dangling from his button hole. Impeccably dressed, they said he was; not your typical down-and-out."

"And what did the papers say about how he ended up in the water? Another accident?"

"There was no evidence to suggest otherwise, apparently. No signs of violence or struggle. The landlord of the Mixer confirmed that Cecil had rather more to drink than usual for a Thursday night but seemed fine when he left the pub. Some of the customers went to the funeral."

"But not Lionel."

"No. Cecil's death brought him a sense of peace, of release, as if a great weight had been lifted from his shoulders. That was how he put it."

"No regrets? I thought he'd known Cecil since they were boys at Broomwood Lodge."

"None that I detected," she said, sliding her empty glass towards him. "None at all."

The café was filling up and conversation becoming difficult. The bubble of complicity had been burst and it was time to leave. As they made their way to the gate to wait for Guy, Hugh said,

"I'm told that Henry Marland remembers you."

"Who?

"He was the archivist at Assendene when the trust was set up in 1989. I gather you gave them some family papers."

"Ah, yes. Nice man. He was very patient, very helpful. Those papers spent years in boxes in my mother's spare room; Assendene seemed the right place for them. They were in a bit of a muddle, I fear. When we were clearing the Camden house, some of the papers that had come to Isabel were mixed up with things that had been Lionel's. No doubt everything was sorted out and catalogued long ago."

Harsh cries, a flash of green as two parakeets flew

low, bringing Hester sharply back to the present. A large car drew up, a door opened. As she was getting in, Hugh said,

"You may like to have this." He gave her the carrier bag in which Lionel's journal had been resting against the leg of a table in the café. "It turned up in a local bookshop."

Seventeen

You got away earlier than I expected," said Kate. "Did she give you time off for good behaviour?"

"It was becoming hard to hear in the café and I'm not sure she had anything else to say."

"What *did* she say?"

"She dipped into the later life of Lionel Pybus, illustrated by drawings and paintings she'd brought with her in a big bag. She was loquaciously selective, as ever. But the thing that seems most certain is the one I understand least."

"You're being cryptic."

"He was clearly a talented artist, and not without admirers in his day, but he's barely known now."

"Isn't that the fate of most creative people? Occasionally, someone is rediscovered and there's a fuss about them for a while."

"Lionel seems to have sought obscurity or, at best, not cared much one way or the other what people thought. It was not a case of struggling to achieve recognition in the face of indifference. The indifference was his own. Hester did try to explain his reluctance to put his head above the parapet."

"Did you give her the journal?"

"As she was leaving. Securely wrapped up to reduce the risk of further discussion. If my theory is correct, she's seen the journal before, of course."

That evening, Sue was catching up with Kate while Hugh was upstairs with the girls. When he came down, she intoned,

"*The child is father to the man.* Who said that? Hopkins or Wordsworth or someone, wasn't it? Anyway, the boy who did the sketches I saw in that old book when I was here last time. Kate says he turned into a proper artist when he grew up."

"I'd say he was already a proper artist as a boy. As an adult, he had various abstract phases, though whether you'd call him a semi-professional artist or an enthusiastic amateur I'm not sure. He taught in art schools for a living."

Hugh fetched his laptop and located the few examples of Lionel's painting he had found before.

"They're restrained, aren't they?" said Sue, after a while. "Rather flat when you think of some of his early sketches, despite the colour. All those clean lines and sharp edges. On the face of it, they're a bit cold or neutral but they're carefully calculated, cleverly thought through. And the way everything seems to interact with everything else. If you ask me, they're the work of a man quietly determined to achieve his objectives and not let anything get in his way."

Hugh wished he'd thought of that. Sue had an unnerving habit of making perceptive comments out of the blue.

"This one's an outlier, though," he said, pointing to the fiery sunset, or whatever it was. "It doesn't seem to fit the pattern of his development at all."

"Unless it pre-dates the abstracts and is one of his first efforts with paint. It's certainly closer in feel to some of the sketches I saw."

Her gaze shifted from the screen to the opposite wall and back and then back to the wall again.

"That picture over there," she said. "Between the bookcase and the fireplace."

"It's an early one of Lucy's. She gave it to us years ago."

"Do you notice a similarity?" she said, passing him the laptop.

"I see what you mean," he said, "but Lionel's own works are reminiscent of other artists. Besides, he died years before she was born."

Lucy's reply was a bit defensive, Hugh thought. He hadn't suggested plagiarism or that her early work was derivative. His email had asked merely whether she had come across the paintings of Lionel Pybus and, if so, whether they had been an influence in the development of her own style. She said she did know of him 'as it happens'. Her father, Raymond Potter, had been one of Lionel's final batch of students before he retired and had long since retired himself. She had grown up with

'Pybus on the walls'. Most of the pictures were now at her parents' house in Spain but she had one or two herself.

'One or two' proved to be half a dozen, if the images attached to the email were anything to go by. They were mostly examples of late Pybus, similar to ones he had seen before, with two exceptions demonstrating that Lionel had lost none of his skills as a draughtsman. A Christmas card in pen and ink: *Greetings from Lionel and Isabel Pybus* above a snow-covered scene, the garden at the back of a house with a snowman centre-stage, footsteps leading off to the right. And another card: *Lionel and Isabel Pybus are moving* showing a Pickfords' van apparently taking the contents of the house at the top to the house at the bottom, giving the address of each. It was the move from Tooting to Camden.

The Tooting house wasn't far from here. He wondered about going to see it. Just out of curiosity. Had Hester known the place when she was a child or been to it since? Or taken Rachel and the others? He reminded himself, yet again, that it was their family history, not his. His involvement was purely…what? He still wasn't sure. Kate was right that they had no idea how much Hester had shared with Rachel, who did not appear to be unduly put out by her mother's latching on to Hugh. 'Spilling the beans', as Hester put it. On the other hand, it did not feel as though she was simply re-running for his benefit things she had been over before.

Eighteen

*I*t was dark when they set out and the girls slept most of the way. Now, as Hugh drove along Beadles Lane, skirting beech woods on one side and ploughed fields on the other, they were prodded and primed by Kate for their imminent arrival at Assendene Court. He turned left at the lodge and took the gently curving drive towards the house. The elms that Lionel had mentioned in his journal had departed long since and the rooks with them.

The day was turning into a fine one and, after a period of recovery in the tea room, there was little resistance to the suggestion of a walk. They chose the Yellow Route, a relatively undemanding stroll across the park and around the lake, with the option of a muddier extension through woods and farmland. 'They' meant Kate and the girls, for Hugh had an appointment with the archivist, Emily Coote, to follow up the conversations they had had on the phone. This was one of the few Saturdays she was on duty.

He knew the way but it felt odd to be taking it as

if nothing had happened the last time he was here. He approached the service block with some diffidence and hesitated before pressing the button of the entry phone at the side entrance. Emily buzzed him through and met him in the corridor at the exact spot that Simon Marmion had wheezed a welcome before leading him to his office.

Emily did not linger as she took him up twisting stairs and along an ill-lit passage to a meeting room in which various items were laid out on a table. She was a small woman in her early thirties, he reckoned, with honey-coloured hair to her shoulders and serious glasses. Her manner was brisk but by no means brusque and she had clearly enjoyed the delving and devilling in which she had been engaged.

Many of the papers concerned the running of the estate, an increasingly depressing account of Assendene's gradual decline after the First World War that culminated in the lock, stock and barrel sale to Clive Paragon. Game books testified to the kind of slaughter that had appalled the young Lionel, though entries tailed off markedly once Giles succeeded Sir Ralph. Of greater interest to Hugh were the visitors' books, kept scrupulously up-to-date until the point at which Giles was forced to leave. He spotted some famous names in the early pages, when the house was in its heyday, later dwindling to a recurrent few, marked with post-it notes inserted by Emily. Lionel and Isabel were frequent visitors, as were their daughter Sophia, and, much later, her own daughter Hester. It was strangely affecting to see Hester's childish handwriting developing in confidence and style over the years.

Emily had been back far enough to find the entries for Lionel's visits in 1902 – 'he seems to have left rather abruptly' – and 1911 – 'strange there should have been such a long gap between them'. She was obviously right to conclude that Lionel's connection with the place long pre-dated his marriage to Isabel, 'presumably through the brother, Freddy'. On the other hand, there was no reason why she should have recognised the name of Cecil Collingwood, though she may have wondered at its repetition in the decade or so before the First World War, first appearing even before that of Lionel Pybus, and its absence afterwards.

Hugh had known something of the look of the family from the photographs reproduced in the guidebook and from the sketches in Lionel's journal. The boxes on the table contained many more photographs, including pictures of staff, estate workers and visitors. Some were formal set-piece affairs, others more relaxed and less obviously posed. Which one, he wondered, was the parlour maid overheard referring to their young guest as 'Master Lionel Piecrust' or Sarah, the housemaid who hoped he would come back? Were those the gardeners who had damped down the remains of the smouldering maze? Could the racy woman next to Lady Assendene be Aunt Violet, making a rare foray from her home in Menton? And the car with the grim-faced chauffeur standing beside it, was that the Daimler in which Lionel had been taken to the station with a bag of cakes?

There were too many photographs to examine properly. The archivist had set aside a selection featuring Lionel, in various combinations of family and others, from his earliest visits to his last. How well his sketches had captured the likeness of the young Isabel, whose warm and intelligent eyes shone through to the end. The one Emily identified as his daughter, Sophia, looked uncannily like Rachel, while the girl pointed out as Hester bore more of a resemblance to Isabel herself.

They were a striking family. But it was the photograph taken on the terrace in 1911 that made a particular impression: a group that included Lionel in cream flannels and striped blazer, looking nervous and out of place next to Freddy's jaunty confidence and charm. And, behind them, a tall, thin young man, a flower of some sort in his button hole, destined to lose his life not on the battlefields of France, like Freddy, but half a century later in a canal in Camden Town.

That – and a photograph of Lionel and Giles, taken some time in the 1950s, standing by the entrance to the walled garden. Lionel looking laidback, untroubled; Giles careworn and crumpled by the burden of the estate.

"You could almost mistake them for brothers, couldn't you," said Emily.

Hugh nodded but kept his thoughts to himself. The resemblance was undeniable. No wonder Hester had ducked the issue of how she was related to Giles.

"You mentioned some curiosities when we spoke on the phone." He glanced at his watch and wondered how the walk was going. They had agreed to rendezvous back in the tea room.

Emily turned and lifted from the top of the cabinet behind her two volumes bound in burgundy leather. The front covers of both bore the emblem of a maze tooled in gold.

"These are rather odd," she said, passing them to him. "One is inscribed 'The Book of Acquisitions', the other 'The Book of Members'. Both beautifully kept. There's obviously an Assendene connection, given the bindings, but their place in the archive is not entirely clear."

A frisson of excitement as he took them and turned the pages of each in turn. The record, when put together, of Freddy's tasks and those charged with carrying them out. Just as Hester had described. And on the title page of each volume, in the bottom right-hand corner, three words: 'The Amber Maze'. She had clearly seen them both.

"Did Hester not explain what they were at the time?"

"She said something about a society in which Freddy and Lionel were involved at Oxford, according to Henry Marland. She was insistent that they be kept with the other family papers, although they appear to relate to the doings of others. There are some press cuttings stuck in the Book of Acquisitions about a gruesome incident on a farm not far from here. At least they help with dates. Pre-First World War, of course, though there are two later insertions at the end of the book."

Hugh flicked through it carefully and removed two further cuttings. One, from 1935, recorded the death of a prominent Member of Parliament and junior Minister at an underground station in central London. The other was a short piece about the drowning of a homeless man over thirty years later. Their connection with the contents of either volume was not stated but, as Emily pointed out, the initials of the unfortunate men tallied with some of those written next to the cuttings about the farmland mutilations; the names could be found in full in the Book of Members. She did not seem to have noticed that one of the names also cropped up in the Assendene visitors' book.

"Looks like this society was engaged in a bit more than japes and dining," said Emily, "but my focus is on the house and family."

"'The Amber Maze'…"

"Appears to be the name of the society. Don't ask me why. I don't think Hester said."

In Emily's office, over a cup of tea, Hugh told her a bit about his previous visit and about the stained-glass window in the pavilion, the image of a maze brilliant in the afternoon sun.

"As if the maze itself was on fire. The gift of an anonymous donor, Simon Marmion told me."

"It's fairly recent," said Emily. "Made and installed in the early 1990s, after the trust took over. But designed rather earlier, I believe."

"Designed for that spot?"

"Looks like it. Pity we don't have the drawings."

"The donor commissioned as well as paid for it?"

"With the trust's agreement. I assume they must have had some idea of what they were getting. Whoever designed the window must have known the place well."

"Your turn," said Kate, after they had trooped round the house. "I'm going to look at the walled garden."

She left Hugh in charge of Eleanor and Rosie. They made their way to the pavilion, ostensibly to look at a display about wildlife in and around the lake. He had with him the photocopy of the plan of the maze found in Lionel's box, the one he had left in his jacket when he had been here before.

While the girls were reading about moorhens, dabchicks and the great crested grebe, he looked up at the stained-glass window. Without the sun directly behind, it looked dull and unremarkable but there was no doubt that it matched the plan he had in his hand, scaled up to fit the space. He could have told Emily, of course, that Lionel had designed the window but he felt somehow that it wasn't for him to do it.

The sudden crash of a door. Eleanor and Rosie ran out shouting,

"We're going to look at the maze."

His protests went unheeded or unheard as they sped past the barrier towards the entrance and disappeared. He ran to the entrance and stopped. He had the plan, he could have followed them and caught up. But the sight of those towering hedges, constricting and confining the narrow path between them, brought it all back. He could not move. How long he stood there he did not know. But eventually the panic subsided and he decided to walk round to the exit to meet them. As he arrived, they burst out breathless and giggling and accused him of cheating.

After lunch, they all went to the shop where Hugh was greeted warmly by the manager, Pamela Quince, who had been at the house when they found Simon Marmion that day. She affected shock and horror when the girls said they had been in the maze and lowered her voice to say to Hugh,

"Between you, me and the gatepost, I think closing the maze to the public was an over-reaction."

"Simon said it was closed as long ago as 2002. Something to do with health and safety."

"There was a minor incident that autumn. A small fire at the centre of the maze. A visitor chose the spot to burn some papers, including a photograph. I don't imagine for one moment that she intended to set light to the hedge; it was easily extinguished. The garden steward and his assistant were a little heavy-handed and, in the scuffle that followed, the statue of Pan was knocked off its plinth and damaged."

"You said 'she'."

"She refused to give her name, I gather, but I recognised her as she was leaving. She had been to Assendene before but I've not seen her since. She was told not to come back; there's no one left but me who would know her now."

"Did she say why she started the fire?"

"She told the steward she was marking a centenary. Of what, she did not say but I had a quiet word with Henry Marland, our archivist at the time. He said it was a hundred years to the day that the original maze was burnt down."

"Curiouser and curiouser. You mentioned a photograph."

"It wasn't destroyed completely. I took the precaution of removing it when I was sent in to clear up the mess. I could see who it was, though he looked younger than his picture in the guide. Just a boy, really. It was Freddy Assendene."

The sign by the gate in the car park fence was barely legible and took some finding. The others were content to stay in the car while he followed the footpath to St Mark's. He entered the churchyard between two yew trees whose canopies had combined to create a short but sinister tunnel that opened among gravestones encrusted with grey-green lichen.

He paused in a patch of sun to take in the stocky church of flint and stone and the arched doorway where Lionel and Isabel had stood on their wedding day in 1920. Inside, the building was cool and quiet and still, a fresh vase of Michaelmas daisies the only clue that anyone else had been here recently. His footsteps echoed on the tiled floor as he made his way to the Assendene family crypt. The heavy oak door at the bottom of the steps was locked. He pulled and twisted and rattled the handle in frustration but remembered where he was. He went back to the wall he had passed. Set in it, rectangular tablets of plain white marble marking the lives of people he had never met but whose names had become familiar. Two tablets were cleaner and crisper than the rest: Giles and Isabel, the last of the Assendenes. They had died only weeks apart.

A double loss. The effect on Lionel could only be imagined. Yet as a Pybus he had no place here; the long years of association with the family, his marriage into it, did not change that. Where he lay, Hester had not said. Just that Lionel had given strict instructions that he was not to be cremated.

Nineteen

I haven't heard much about Isabel," said Kate. They were sitting after supper that evening, Bill Evans playing softly in the background. "Considering the part she must have played in his life."

"Hester said she was the brightest of the siblings but was not brought up to have expectations and no one had any of her. She didn't go to school, had a governess at Assendene and drifted round France and Italy before training to be a nurse."

"And then the dutiful daughter became the dutiful wife. But what did she actually do?"

"Had a daughter herself, went back to nursing, and tried to get Lionel to be more assertive in selling his paintings. Even went to galleries herself to drum up interest in his work. And Emily Coote said she taught French at WEA – Workers' Educational Association – classes for years in both Tooting and Camden. They stayed regularly with her Aunt Violet in Menton before the war."

He leaned forward and picked up the envelope lying

on the coffee table. He slid out a diary. It was about the size of a paperback book, its spine faded, the boards still fresh and crisp, grey watered silk shimmering in the light of the standard lamp. And on the front, four numerals in gold gleamed invitingly: 1 9 5 2.

They had been in a box, the diaries, stretching forward and back, uniform in size and colour, marking the passing of the years. A tempting prospect. But even Emily had done no more than sample, dipping largely at random. Isabel's hand, she said, unchanged from first to last, neat, sensible, with the hint of a flourish suppressed. But she had read enough to lift out this one for Hugh, present it to him like a school prize for diligence and hard work, suggest he look through it at a better moment. As long as he promised to give it back.

The diary opened, as if of its own accord, at the page marked by a thin silk ribbon. The entry for a day in November 1952. He began to read in silence; it was a record, it turned out, of reflections as well as events. And then he passed the diary to Kate and asked her to read aloud.

I thought Lionel was behaving oddly but I did not expect what I found on the breakfast room table. A large bunch of chrysanthemums, russet and orange, loosely arranged in that art deco vase Giles gave us last Christmas. Poor Giles; he looks more like Lionel every year. Or should that be poor Lionel? I've never quite decided.

There were two small sketches leaning against the vase.

Both, of course, by Lionel, the frames identical. Lionel by the dresser, dancing from one foot to the other like an over-excited schoolboy. The sketch on the left, he said, he made of me on his first visit to Assendene. I could only have been nine or ten. I wondered how many drawings he must have done at the time: I have seen others before but not this one. The sketch on the right was the one he insisted on doing in the drawing room yesterday but would not let me see. He must have put it in the frame after I went to bed.

I disgraced myself by blubbing and broke down completely when he said today was our fiftieth anniversary. Fifty years to the day that we first met in that damp November of 1902 and I brought him ink from the schoolroom. He said he knew straightaway that he would marry me, even if a gap of eighteen years was a little longer than he had anticipated. I said I had felt just the same – on both counts – but had feared, after the fire, I would never see him again. Perhaps I came to have other ambitions too, not least for him. I have not given up hope that his talent will be recognised by more than the loyal few.

He produced a handkerchief in the manner of a conjurer for me to wipe my eyes. A clean white one, not the usual rag smelling of turpentine. Tomorrow, he said, we would be joined by Sophia and little Hester on a trip to Assendene but tonight we would be off to Mayfair for dinner at the Mirabelle. (I do like lobster and champagne!)

And then he brought from another pocket a lump of amber. He placed it in the palm of my hand. It was warm to the touch and silky smooth. I had not seen it in many years, had forgotten it, assumed it was lost. But it was unmistakably the same piece of Baltic amber given me by my governess, Miss

Makepeace, whose brother had brought it back from Lithuania.
In the middle, a fly preserved intact and trapped forever. Freddy
was much taken with it, said the colour reminded him of the
maze in the afternoon sun. Then he spoiled it by laughing
and saying what if someone were trapped in the maze forever.
Would they be preserved untouched?

Lionel said I placed it in his palm all those years ago, a
piece of Assendene to keep with him. And it seems he did,
locked in that box of his along with who knows what else?
I've never seen inside.

"The Assendene effect," said Kate, resting the diary on
her lap. "You'd better watch out. It's like a permanent
marker. Indelible."

"Forever amber, eh? Maybe it works both ways.
Damaged or disregarded in life, given a second chance
in death."

Twenty

*H*ugh and Lucy had the same thought. In the months that followed they could no longer remember which of them had set the ball rolling. Either way, they agreed that, after half a century, another retrospective of the work of Lionel Pybus would not be premature.

How to go about it? The gallery at Toad Books was a possibility but the space was limited and its focus was on local artists. Anthony said the Tooting connection might help but suggested that, if the objective was to ensure Lionel finally had the recognition he deserved, a larger and more prominent gallery would be a better bet. Always assuming such a gallery could be persuaded to run with the idea.

And then there was the question of the paintings themselves. Lucy was prepared to lend hers and her father likewise, subject to the logistics of transporting them from Spain. But it needed more than the offerings of two Potters, which were representative only of late Pybus in any case. The retrospective, they felt, should have examples of the full range of Lionel's work, showing not only the development of his style as a painter but also his skills as a draughtsman. A trawl of galleries and private collectors would be required but the starting point had to be the family and, specifically, Hester.

In the Lakeside Café, she had produced a small selection of pictures from her bag but how many more did she have and would she be prepared to expose them to public gaze? She had not stood in the way of the Black Box exhibition in 1970; perhaps some of the paintings sold at that event could be tracked down and shown again, preferably the right way up.

As he was putting the lights on the Christmas tree at number twelve Falstaff Road, Hugh pondered how best to broach the subject with Hester. A thundering on the front door snapped him back. It was Guy Broadbent, holding a package and looking faintly embarrassed.

The package had a Father Christmas label of the sort he remembered from his childhood. He was, however, instructed to open it now. Guy stuttered that it was a present from Hester, who apologised for not thanking him sooner for 'the book', as he put it, that Hugh had given her in the car and for putting up with her maundering over the last few weeks.

Brown paper gave way to bubble wrap and thence to tissue paper. And then the object was revealed: a magnificent early Pybus, the image itself roughly A4 in size. Not the one he had seen over the café table but with similar divided circles of colour and, in the bottom righthand corner, 'LP 1922'. A note fluttered to the floor. He picked it up and turned it over:

To Hugh from Hester
With gratitude and good wishes.
Dorothy said you were a good listener.

His response was uncharacteristically effusive, which seemed to embarrass Guy even more. Hugh said he would write to thank her. He was uncertain how much Guy knew about the Pybus connection and whether he might have views about Hester giving away one of Lionel's pictures rather than keeping it in the family. He put the question anyway, the one that had been troubling him when he was doing the lights. Guy's advice was to wait until the New Year before sounding her out about a retrospective. The question did not appear to surprise him at all.

The Cork Street gallery of Bainbridge and Murray had not joined the recent exodus of galleries from this part of Mayfair, buoyant sales having enabled them to absorb the rent rises that had forced others to flee. For the time being. It remained to be seen how long they could maintain a foothold. There were whispers of redevelopment, of contingency plans, of options examined and rejected or put on hold, of an eventual move to South Kensington or even the East End.

None of this dampened the enthusiasm of Paul Barnard, a director of the firm, when Lucy got in touch. Paul had arranged the successful exhibition of her own paintings at the gallery a few years ago, followed by another at the Galerie Marion Ducasse in Paris some months later. He knew very little about Lionel Pybus or his work, he said, but the images attached to her email persuaded him that the idea of a retrospective was at least worth exploring.

Paul had the resources and the contacts to progress the research and track down examples of Lionel's output, with the online assistance of Raymond Potter and the active support of Hester Badingham. She produced more pictures at a session with Paul at The Old Rectory, facilitated by Hugh and Lucy, at which Guy and Rachel were also present. Hester had finally agreed to move in with them properly and taken her possessions out of storage.

Paul also had the good fortune to bump into Jeremy Brandon one Friday evening in the courtyard of Burlington House, home to the Royal Academy. Jeremy was a college friend of Paul's and great-grandson of Charles Brandon, whom, it emerged, had accumulated a collection of Pybus paintings. These had passed to Jeremy; he invited Paul to come and see them in his flat overlooking Battersea Park.

The taxi disgorged four Mullions outside the premises of Bainbridge and Murray. A large banner told passers-by that the next four weeks were devoted to:

Lionel Pybus
(1890-1969)
A Retrospective and A Reappraisal

The exhibition opened the following day; tonight was the Private View. The gallery was already crowded as they penetrated the brilliant white cube and wove towards the reception desk. Whether Dido, part-obscured by an enormous autumn arrangement, remembered them from Lucy's event was unclear. A cheery greeting for gallery visitors was no doubt par for the course.

A pile of catalogues leaned dangerously on a side table. Hugh had one at home but took another for Kate. It was an impressive document, profusely illustrated in colour. It included a lengthy biographical note about the artist that he had contributed himself, in collaboration with Hester and Raymond Potter and drawing, with the trust's permission, on the guide to Assendene Court and on its archives. A closer look at the Book of Members had revealed Freddy's estimation of Lionel's performance as Keeper: *Reliable but lacking initiative or imagination. Malleable. Sketches do the job proficiently enough; he is not lacking in talent but better advised to stick to scribbling.* This assessment was not included in the catalogue.

However, a place was found for a brief anecdote contributed by Raymond in the section on Lionel's career as art tutor. Describing him as 'a quietly inspirational teacher', affable and popular, Raymond recalled an incident in which a student inadvertently set light to a watercolour sketch he had put to dry on the stove in the corner of the studio. The normally placid tutor had screamed at the unfortunate student to douse the flames, and rushed from the room. He was found on a bench in the corridor shaking and sweating profusely. Lionel returned the next morning as if nothing had happened.

Hugh and Kate lifted glasses of champagne from the drinks table – the girls were confined to sparkling elderflower, which they told the man from the *Standard* was 'really champagne' – and braved the throng. The pictures were exciting a lot of interest, though it was hard to get near them. Paul had done a good job in putting together a comprehensive and balanced survey of Lionel's work. There were no red stickers; none of the pictures was for sale. A few of the owners, Paul said, had taken some persuading to lend. Not so, Jeremy Brandon, free with items from his collection and offering his firm's generous sponsorship too. Nor Hugh himself, whose sole Pybus, the present from Hester, was prominent among the early works.

He spotted Lucy deep in conversation with Anthony Buffo in front of vignettes Lionel had designed for a poetry magazine in the late 1930s. Her short black hair was enlivened by a streak of magenta. Nearby, Paul, tanned and relaxed as ever in the familiar linen suit, was talking to a group of journalists while his partner, Clare Mallory, whom Hugh had last seen at Lucy's show, swiped some canapés from a passing tray. Next to her, a woman in a yellow dress stood transfixed by a series of flower studies in pen and ink that he was unaware Lionel had done. A little further along it was not so much the pictures as Hester's pantaloons that claimed attention. She was clearly enjoying it.

"She threatened the full Uzbek," breathed Rachel, glad to find a familiar face; Guy had been deputed to attend the school concert with Willow and Matilda. "I put my foot down. And that man she's with, Jeremy something; she's talking to him about his great-grandfather. Apparently, she met him in 1970 at Lionel's last retrospective. Sometimes, I wonder whether I know my mother at all."

In a second, quieter, room Paul was standing in front of two pictures displayed under the cryptic heading 'Outliers'. He was with a youngish couple whom he introduced to Hugh as Colin Mallory, brother of Clare, and his partner, Bryony. Her long golden hair shone under the gallery spots, presenting a striking contrast to Colin's unruly mop of brown. The pair looked vaguely familiar but Hugh could not think why.

"I was just saying that these two paintings don't fit the pattern of the rest. Neither is signed or dated but their provenance is reliable. The top one appears to predate the abstracts that are the Pybus trademark, making it the earliest picture in the show."

It was the watercolour in oranges and reds that Hugh had first seen on the website of Gavels, the auctioneers.

"It is said to be a sunset but I'm not so sure."

"Looks like a massive fire," said Colin. "A conflagration."

"You may be right," said Paul. "You can almost warm your hands by it. Whereas the bottom one is much more muted and entirely different in style. It is thought to be one of Lionel's last paintings. The title on the back is 'Just Deserts'. Make of that what you will."

The picture comprised a series of superimposed images in shades of grey appearing to depict a man falling towards an area of darkness: perhaps an abyss, perhaps nothing, perhaps water, perhaps simply representing oblivion. The man's features were indistinct. It looked vaguely Cubist or Futurist in inspiration.

"If you ask me, it owes something to that painting by Marcel Duchamp," said Bryony. "'Nude Descending a Staircase'. It featured in one of the episodes of *Theft*."

That's where he had seen her! She was in that television series about stolen art treasures. But what about Colin? Was he an actor too?

Paul agreed about the Duchamp inspiration – or pastiche – but remained puzzled about the picture. He did not comment on the small pink dot recurring in roughly the area of the man's buttonhole and neither did Hugh.

Twenty-one

*H*ugh read and re-read the wadge of press cuttings Paul had sent him. 'A compelling exhibition', declared one; 'a revelation', said another; 'establishes the reputation of a neglected genius', proclaimed a third. Others saw Lionel Pybus (dubbed 'the Tooting Kandinsky' by a south London paper) as a highly skilled imitator rather than an original talent, with comparisons variously to Robert and Sonia Delaunay, Paul Klee, Piet Mondrian and Ben Nicholson, depending on the period of Pybus that had caught their eye. Many referred to the skill and control of his compositions and his sense of colour ('a superb colourist') and to the quality of his draughtsmanship, as exemplified by the flower studies ('reminiscent of John Nash').

There was some speculation about why the man was an unknown (no paper had carried an obituary when he died). Most concluded, like the catalogue, that Lionel was a modest man who shunned the limelight rather than adopting the harsher line that his neglect was largely self-inflicted. Little attention was paid to the

1970 retrospective, of which no reports from the time could be found. Any reviews had slipped from sight, much like the Black Box Gallery itself.

Despite the warmth and enthusiasm of the response, and praise for Paul in curating it, Hugh had picked up a sense of resentment among some owners that the secret of Pybus was out, as if the artist was as much their property as the paintings. If Lionel's belated recognition increased the value of the pictures they already had on their walls it scuppered the chances of picking up any more for a song.

Hugh himself was ambivalent about the intrusion into Lionel's quiet life, despite the part he had played in bringing the Pybus story to public view. Or perhaps because of it. He looked again at the tender sketches of the Assendenes and Lionel's own family reproduced in the catalogue. They included one of Lady Assendene ('LP 1911') that put beyond doubt that the drawing added at the end of Lionel's journal was a picture of her rather than Isabel. He had taken the precaution of photocopying it before giving the journal to Hester.

And then there was 'Just Deserts'. A work of observation or imagination? One or two reviewers echoed Bryony's comment about the Duchamp painting and saw Lionel's version simply as a witty allusion. She and Colin Mallory had difficulty in leaving the room in which the picture was displayed when the girls, Eleanor and Rosie, ambushed them with squeals of 'Tommy Tuppence', a character Colin had played in a children's programme some years ago. Perhaps that was where Hugh had seen him.

★

Kate found the postcard, sandwiched between a bulb catalogue and a clutch of menus for local takeaways. It was from Hester, the card he had given her when they first met, showing the maze at Assendene in about 1900.

> *I enjoyed the Cork Street beano. Quite a fuss*
> *in the papers afterwards! I've been in touch with*
> *Henry Marland, who thinks I can safely return*
> *to Assendene. I'm off there with Rachel and the*
> *girls next week. They've never seen the place.*
> *And the trust has decided to re-open the maze!*
> *You probably know all this; you always were*
> *one step ahead.*

Also by Christopher Bowden

The Blue Book

Fear death by water. D.

The discovery of a cryptic note hidden inside a second-hand book sends thirty-something Hugh Mullion on an obsessive search for its previous owner. Hugh uncovers secrets that have lain hidden for sixty years and turn upside down his views of personal identity and the certainty of the past. Along the way, Hugh learns more about himself and what he really wants from his relationship with his partner, Kate – and about the puzzling disappearances of Anthony Buffo, in whose shop Hugh found the book that changed everything.

"…an intriguing and affecting story written with élan… the kind of book that readers love."

The Yellow Room

When Jessica Tate finds an old country house guide in a box after her grandmother's funeral she is drawn into a mystery that has remained unsolved for over half a century and is set to change her life forever. Intrigued by the house and the family that lived there, she is propelled into a world of disappearances and deceptions, eventually unlocking the secret of the Yellow Room itself.

As the shadows lift, a picture emerges of a landed family fighting to stem the decline in its fortunes in a post-war world in which Britain's own role is steadily declining.

"…a rare glimpse into our recent history, far too rarely plundered by modern novelists, and deftly done." *Andrew Marr*

"A novel as intriguing as the house at its heart. I loved it." *Julian Fellowes*

"…quintessentially English…an intriguing book, full of family mysteries and deception." *Oxford Times*

The Red House

Her face was thinner than it used to be, tauter somehow, almost gaunt, and the eyes seemed troubled. The hair, once long and flowing, was cut roughly short. Almost hacked, he thought. Yet it was surely her...

When Colin Mallory sees a sketch of a young actress he once knew on display in the local market, memories of their past together are brought back sharply to the surface. Alarmed by her distressed appearance, Colin is propelled on a search that draws him into the nightmare world of 'the group' and the sinister influence that threatens to control him too.

This is an engrossing story of artifice and hidden secrets, rich with theatrical detail and a cast of compelling characters.

"Very entertaining, cleverly constructed and expertly paced. I thoroughly enjoyed it." *Sir Derek Jacobi*

The Green Door

BEATRICE NEWTON
1876 – 1887
She fell asleep too soon

Clare Mallory has a Victorian mourning locket with the photograph of a girl and a curl of her hair. When Clare loses the locket in a fortune-teller's tent her quest to find it draws her into a dark episode of the family's past and the true circumstances of the girl's untimely death at Danby Hall, her Norfolk home.

The locket has been taken by the fortune-teller herself, sensing a troubled history and danger ahead. But her attempts to understand the warning signs release forces long held at bay. Events of the past seep into the present until the reappearance of a man who vanished from Danby Hall in 1887 threatens not only her life but Clare's too.

"Draws the reader in immediately and has all the elements of an intriguing mystery. In short, a page-turner. The heroine, Clare, is engaging and Madame Pavonia a suitably exotic yet credibly mundane fortune teller, and throughout there is a nice balance of the chillingly supernatural with a sharply observed contemporary England peopled by vividly painted characters...some lovely idiosyncratic touches and descriptions." *Shena Mackay*

"Subtly written but still a page-turner, it is a spine-chillingly enjoyable read." *The Lady*

"...strange but appealing..." *Herald Scotland*

"...an interesting and unusual story. I enjoyed the blend of mystery and supernatural. It's quite the page-turner but it doesn't neglect character and detail. Absorbing and evocative, *The Green Door* is a truly enjoyable read." *The Bookbag*

The Purple Shadow

In the years before the war, Sylvie Charlot was a leading light in Paris fashion with many friends among musicians, artists and writers. Now she is largely forgotten. Spending time in Paris during a break in his acting career, Colin Mallory sees a striking portrait of Sylvie. Some think it is a late work by Édouard Vuillard but there is no signature or documentary evidence to support this view.

The picture has some unusual qualities, not least the presence of a shadow of something that cannot be seen. Perhaps the picture was once larger. Colin feels an odd sense of connection with Sylvie, who seems to be looking at him, appealing to him, wanting to tell him something. Despite a warning not to pursue his interest in her portrait, he is determined to find out more about the painting, who painted it, and why it was hidden for many years.

Colin's search takes him back to the film and theatre worlds of Paris and London in the 1930s – and to a house in present-day Sussex. As he uncovers the secrets of Sylvie's past, her portrait seems to take on a life of its own.

"A compelling read. You're drawn into the narrative immediately by the vivid description of a startlingly captivating painting and, as a reader, you're as invested in getting to the bottom of the mystery as the main character is. Bowden is a sharp observer and I loved his descriptions of Paris and London and Sussex and the people who live in both city and country. The novel also spends time describing the lives of jobbing actors and the British film industry in the 1930s. This may be fiction but you feel, as you read, that it comes from a place of knowledge." *The Bookbag*

"Full of idiosyncratic touches and descriptions, this is a story that will keep you guessing." *France magazine*

"Christopher Bowden has again created an intriguing, literary tale with a well-drawn cast of characters. Actor Colin Mallory from *The Red House* can't help but investigate a mysterious painting. The descriptive quality of the writing takes you to the back streets of Paris, and lets you really feel you are solving the mystery hand in hand with Colin." *Lovereading*